I0835645

Edited by: Partners In Crime Book Services
Cover design and formatting by: Rebecca Poole of Dreams2media

TL SHIVELY

Dedication

This Trilogy is dedicated to my husband, Paul Bush. He was the one who vied for the trilogy, and the one who helped me bring it to you. He is my biggest cheerleader, fan, and he'll tell you that he is just the muscle. I'm here to tell you that he is much more.

Thank you for all that you do for me, Paul. I love you!

Chapter 1

"Hey, Spider!"

Calista looked over and smiled. Solen lay on a blanket beside her, propped on his side with one leg crossed over the other. He leaned on his elbow, chin resting in his palm, and grinned at her. With a playful tug, he pulled on a strand of her hair.

She turned her gaze outward, eyes widening as she took in their surroundings. They were in the forest of the Aggies on Ara. Colors bloomed all around them; vivid, radiant, alive. A stark contrast from the last time she'd stood on Ara. The trees no longer looked pale and withered; instead, they thrummed with vibrant life, their aromatic fragrance thick in the air.

"Have I finally left you speechless?"

Calista turned back to Solen, her lips curling into a soft smile in answer to his teasing grin. "If I'm dreaming," she said, "I never want to wake up."

"But you have to."

Her brow furrowed. "Why?"

"You have to go home."

"What?" She shook her head in confusion.

"It's time to go home, Spider."

Her heart tightened at his words. "I don't want to. I want to stay here with you."

"Spider!"

The tranquility shattered.

The vibrant forest of the Aggies faded into chaos, swallowed by the memory of the battlefield on Ara; the day she lost Solen. Explosions rang throughout the air, ones she relived in her nightmares. She no longer lay on a blanket but stood frozen behind a line of boulders, surrounded by the sounds of war. Her body tensed. Her dream had turned into her nightmare.

"Spider! Watch out!" Solen's voice called out once more as she whispered a desperate prayer to wake up before her heart broke all over again.

Suddenly he was there, he grabbed her and spun them around before he pressed her against the far side of a boulder. "That was close, Spider. Can't have you getting hurt."

Not those words again.

Calista started to shake as the world tilted and time slowed. A blinding flash of light surrounded them just as Solen turned back toward the fight. The moment stretched, it unfolded like a scene from a movie. She reached out for him, to try to pull him back, but, like before, she was too late.

Solen looked at her in surprise, just like before. Then he collapsed to his knees in her arms.

"Solen! NOOOOO!"

Calista woke with a scream, drenched in cold sweat. She sat at the edge of the bed and buried her face in her hands; her cheeks wet with tears. That nightmare, the same nightmare, haunted her nightly. The day she lost Solen replayed with painful precision. His death still pierced her, even after all this time. She had lost Draken too, but it was Solen, her soulmate, who had left a wound that refused to close.

Yet something was different tonight. She'd never dreamed of lying with him in the forests of Ara before. That part was new.

Movement caught her eye. She turned to see Scratch watching her with concern. Her little eight-legged best friend who had befriended her as a child. She reached out to gently stroke his head and offered a tired sigh. "Hey there, little guy. Sorry to have worried you." He tilted his head at her, and she gave a weak nod. "Same dream. It'll be nice to be home, little fella."

Calista's frown deepened. In the dream, Solen had told her to go home. That had never happened before. Maybe it was because they'd only just decided to return to Atlantis a few days ago. Maybe her mind was trying to prepare her.

Calista shook her head, trying to clear it. Swallowing hard, she rose to her feet. "Let's go get something to drink. No going back to sleep now."

Scratch leapt to her shoulder and nestled into the

crook of her neck. She leaned her cheek against his soft fur. He'd once lived in a pendant around her neck, kept in stasis by Zeus himself. The Ancients had nearly drained his life, but Zeus had made him immortal when Calista was a child, ensuring he could survive. Solen's final act had been to bring her little friend back to life, telling her it was a gift he could only give to his true-life partner, with Ara's blessing.

She thought of that often. Solen's last kindness. His love.

With a wave of her hand, her door slid silently shut behind her. Barefoot, she padded down the hallway, careful not to disturb the others in the sleeping crew quarters. She couldn't remember the last full night of rest she had since the battle of Ara. Since they'd begun their quest to find the Ancients' Queen. Every night, she saw Solen fall. Every night, she woke up screaming.

Thankfully, the soundproofing in the crew quarters kept the others from hearing. She didn't want them worrying; it might distract them from the mission.

Now that they decided to return to Atlantis, Calista felt something she hadn't in a long time: hope. After years of hunting the Ancients and their Queen with no success, the thought of seeing home and family again felt like a warm beacon. A brief pause before they resumed their pursuit.

But there was one thing she wasn't looking forward to: facing Draken's family.

Draken's wife would have to be told that he wasn't coming home, that he gave his life to protect them, mostly to protect Kaine. How do you tell a young son that his father is gone? To say he'll always be with you sounds so hollow. She knew how empty those words could sound. She had lived that emptiness.

Calista moved through the corridors like a ghost, her thoughts so heavy they dulled her senses. Pain and memories swirled through her head, muting everything around her as if she were moving underwater.

Her hand hovered over the mess hall door when a voice stopped her.

"You should be sleeping. There's no telling what we might face tomorrow, and we'll need you at your best."

Calista paused, her brow knitting at the familiar tone. Livinia. And from the sound of it, this wasn't the first time she'd said those words. Livinia rarely let emotion touch her voice. She kept herself as closed off as her expression; calm, cold, unreadable. But now... there was something in her tone. Just the faintest waver. Concern, maybe.

Calista wasn't the only one awake.

A beat later, Rikar answered. "I can't sleep, Liv. Every night, I see Draken dying all over again. I see him rushing to save Kaine; see the energy the Ancients stole from me rip through his chest."

Calista's breath hitched. The tightness in her chest coiled like a vice.

"He died for that idiot," Rikar growled. "And Kaine still charges into battle like my brother's death meant nothing." The pain and rage in his voice filled the room. Calista could feel it leaking through the walls, heavy as grief.

"Kaine is a warrior. He could no more sit on the sidelines than you could," Livinia replied evenly. "In the years we've fought the Ancients, he's more than redeemed himself for what happened on that starship. A starship I was the reason you were even on."

"Are you trying to make me mad at you?" Rikar's response mirrored Calista's own surprise.

"No. I'm stating facts," Livinia said. "You want someone to blame. If that's the case, you should be just as angry with me."

A growl followed; low, half amused, half frustrated. Calista recognized it. That strange, begrudging affection that had grown between the stoic assassin and the wounded warrior. Somehow, Rikar and Livinia had become a pair. A dark, deadly, emotionally stunted pair, but a pair all the same.

She was grateful they didn't flaunt it. Livinia didn't seem capable of sappiness, and Rikar had enough baggage to drown in. Livinia once told her that Rikar made sense for her because he was a warrior too. Practical, logical. But Calista had seen the way Livinia sometimes looked at him, how her armor cracked when no one else was watching.

"Fine," Rikar muttered. "Kaine's redeemed himself. He's not the one I'm angry at. But neither are you."

"Where are you going?" Livinia's voice followed the sound of footsteps.

Calista slipped silently away from the door, disappearing into the shadows just as Rikar emerged with Livinia on his heels.

"Back to bed," he said. "You're right. If I don't sleep, I'm no use when I'm needed."

"Of course I'm right," she replied, and a moment later, the sound of a soft smack and Rikar's chuckle echoed faintly down the corridor. Each day, Livinia changed; just a little. The hard shell cracked. Sometimes, Calista thought she might've seen her smile.

Calista leaned her head back against the cool steel wall, taking a long breath before pushing away and walking on. Her thirst vanished, replaced by the weight of what she'd heard. It wasn't just her haunted by loss. Everyone on this ship carried scars.

As she passed an open doorway, a movement caught her eye.

Cellica spun in the middle of her room, dancing in one of her garish, frilly outfits. Calista shook her head. Cellica was the reason they flew this larger vessel now. The old ship didn't have enough room for her routines, so she'd found a new one, somehow, and made it theirs. Calista didn't ask how she'd managed the trade. When Cellica wanted something, she got it.

Her fingertips skimmed the sleek metal walls as she walked, thinking about Kaine, Allen, Vester, Clori, Stryx, Bern, Arlo, Tanis, and Lissy. The original crew. All still there, working together to take down the Ancients. But their family had grown since leaving Ara, Cellica wasn't the only new crew member they had welcomed aboard.

John, a towering, plushy bear of a being, had joined them after they'd liberated him from an Ancient prison. He could shift his size at will but preferred to keep his massive form, claiming it was "cozy."

And then there was Bastion, their Aggie stowaway.

He'd hidden in a cargo bay, which he'd since transformed into a lush arboretum that mirrored the forests of Ara. Flowers, food crops, even rare herbs grew in that space now. By the time they discovered him, it was too late, he'd already become one of them. They'd sent word to his family to let them know he was safe.

Calista smiled faintly at that thought as she waved open the door to the dining room. Smaller than the mess hall, it had no kitchen access but was stocked with drinks and comfortable seating.

Calista pulled a chilled bottle of water from a cooling unit, a "refrigerator," if she remembered the Earth term, and curled into a chair with Scratch on her lap. As she sipped, her thoughts drifted again. She wished it was that Earth drink she once tried, something called a John Stahle. Bitter and sweet and comforting.

Outside the skyport, what the crew insisted on calling

the window, the stars spun in silence. Cold. Endless. She stared out at them, her body still, her thoughts loud.

Only one word echoed in her heart.

Vengeance.

"Don't you ever sleep?"

Calista turned. Allen stood nearby, arms crossed, concern etched across his face.

"Of course. I just needed a drink." She raised the water as proof.

"You do know there are surveillance recorders in all the common rooms, right? You and Rikar are practically regulars during off-hours."

Caught. Her lips pressed into a tight line.

"It's fine, I get it," Allen said softly. "I miss him too."

She stared down into the bottle, knuckles whitening. Her voice came low, brittle. "Do you dream of him?"

"Often." He nodded. "But I also sleep more than you."

Calista shot him a glare. She had no comeback, because he was right.

"Solen wouldn't want this, Calista," he said. "He wouldn't want you mourning like this."

Since Solen's death, no one had called her Spider. No one dared. That name belonged to him, something sacred between them. And without him, it felt hollow.

Calista swallowed hard. The anger surged behind her ribs like a tide she couldn't hold back.

"I know what he wanted," she snapped. "But I also

know I can't control how I feel. No one can. All I can do is live, and that's what I'm doing."

"Are you sure?"

She raised a brow, but didn't respond. Arguing with Allen was pointless. He reminded her too much of Solen, especially when he pissed her off.

"I wonder if your family would agree," he mused aloud, tilting his head.

"Why wouldn't they?" Her posture stiffened. The words came like a challenge.

Allen shrugged. "I guess we'll find out soon." He turned to leave. "Stryx says we should be ready to fold into Earth's solar system in the next few days. Assuming he can keep your brother off the bridge."

Calista scowled. "Eon's just curious. He didn't mean any harm."

"His curiosity nearly dropped us into an uncalculated fold."

Her glare deepened. "What happened to the kid who wanted to storm an Ancient warship just to fight alongside his brother? You follow rules now. Regulations. Always toeing the line. I'm not complaining, it's been useful, but I miss that wild streak."

Allen turned back, his expression unreadable. But his eyes gleamed. "That kid lost his world and his brother." His voice dropped. "He took off with a crew just as broken as he is. And he swore not to dishonor his brother's memory by doing something stupid that could cost the one person he loved." He lingered a moment, looking at her with something unspoken behind his eyes.

Grief.

Admiration.

Maybe something more.

But whatever he was about to say, he didn't. Instead, he gave her a small, sad smile and turned to go. The door shut behind him with a soft, mechanical hiss.

"Thought I'd find you here."

Calista turned. Kaine stood in the doorway, arms crossed, eyes steady on her. His tone was casual, but concern crept beneath it. "When was the last time you got a good night's sleep?"

She glanced down at the shimmering green liquid in her mug. Steam curled up in lazy spirals, carrying the earthy, spiced scent of Bastion's herbal brew. Pulled from plants grown in his arboretum, it was meant to clear the mind and invigorate the spirit, a distant cousin to Earth's coffee. Bastion called it Zazzy juice.

Calista held up the mug, attempting a light tone. "Who needs sleep when you've got Zazzy juice?" The words fell flat under the weight of her exhaustion, landing in a sigh.

"You need rest, Calista," Kaine said. His voice remained gentle, but there was steel behind the words. "You can't face the queen at half-strength. Solen told you to live. This," he gestured to her, hunched and weary in the dim light, "this isn't living."

Her gaze sharpened. "Did Allen snitch on me?" It had been a few days ago that Allen was standing in that same spot, giving her the same lecture.

"Snitch?" Kaine blinked, puzzled.

"Tattled? Narced? Squealed? Finked?" She sighed when confusion still clouded his face. "Did Allen tell you about the nightmares?"

"No." His brow lifted. "Is that why you haven't been sleeping?"

"If he didn't tell you... then how did you know?" Her voice edged with suspicion.

Kaine huffed a quiet laugh. "It's not exactly a secret. Everyone knows. You sit here every night, staring out the skyport like you're waiting for ghosts." He tilted his head. "Lack of sleep dulls your senses. If someone attacked, you wouldn't even see it coming."

Her brows drew together. "Who would attack me? We're among friends."

"Just like you were back on Ara?"

Her spine straightened. "Are you trying to make me paranoid?"

"I'm trying to make you careful." His expression softened, but his voice didn't waver. "Your well-being matters just as much as this mission."

Calista didn't respond. She bit her lip and looked away, tension coiling in her shoulders. Since Solen's death, Kaine had stepped in, quietly but unmistakably, as her protector. She and Rikar barely spoke anymore, their connection frayed by grief. Kaine had filled that gap without asking, and she hadn't questioned it. Until now.

She opened her mouth, but he cut in.

"We're folding in less than an hour," he said. "Time to head to the stability pods."

"Already?" The days had blurred together, slipping past without shape or meaning. She frowned and stood, dropping the empty mug into the cleaning bin.

"Calista."

She paused at the door and glanced back.

"We're all here for you," he said. "Everyone on this ship. We're your friends. Let us help you."

Her mouth quirked into a tired, uneven smile, more shadow than humor. "How can you help me," she said softly, "when I don't even know how to help myself?"

Without looking back, she slipped into the corridor, her steps taking her toward the pods and, hopefully, a dreamless rest.

CHAPTER 2

"It's so nice to have you home." Malis smiled, pulling Calista into another hug before stretching on tiptoe to ruffle Eon's hair. He now towered over both of them. When they first left Atlantis, Eon had kept the form of a youngster even though he was centuries old. Now, his form was of a young man. Though, a young man who has seen more than most. "You've grown into a very handsome young man."

Eon gave a half-hearted smile before lifting his mother into a tight hug. She patted his arm, then nodded toward the open doorway. "You'd better go see your grandparents before they wonder if you've forgotten them. Calista and I will follow soon."

As Eon nodded and walked off, Malis gently tugged Calista over to the nearest chaise lounge. They sat together, Malis tucked her legs under herself and leaned over to brush a strand of hair behind Calista's ear.

Calista frowned as she glanced toward the door. "Aren't we going to Grandma and Grandpa's?"

"We will," Malis said softly. "But first, I want to talk to my daughter. I see that sadness in your eyes, tucked behind the armor you've built. What happened, sweetheart?"

Calista inhaled shakily. Scratch, as if sensing her tension, moved on his many legs to touch her neck in a comforting caress. She had thought the tears were long gone. So many years had passed. But now, with her mother beside her, she realized just how deeply she missed the gentle perception of her presence.

The dam broke. She collapsed into her mother's arms and told her everything.

The journey. The beauty of Ara. The Champions and the battles. Lizbet's deal. Malis's arms tightened at the mention of Livinia capturing her and Rikar, and a soft gasp escaped her when Calista described Draken's death; his final words, the love he confessed, and the silence that followed when Calista told her what happened between her and Rikar. Her mother didn't speak then. Suspiciously quiet.

Calista lifted her head. Her cheeks were sticky with tears. "You don't seem surprised," she said, wiping her face.

"I already knew how Draken felt about you," Malis admitted gently.

"You knew?" Calista's chest tightened. "Why didn't you tell me?"

"Draken swore us to secrecy. He didn't want to disrupt your life. We argued, told him he should tell you, but in the end, it was his choice; and we respected that." Malis sighed. "We had hoped that eventually, you two would be able to get past all the little blockades and get together. But, you would barely come home," when Calista opened her mouth to apologize, her mother held up a hand to silence her. "No apologies, just trying to explain. You were barely home and then eventually him and Kimi started their relationship. So, we saw no reason to upset either one of you by breaking a promise."

Calista's lips twisted into a half-resigned frown. "I can see your point. I just... I can't believe I was that blind."

"Don't blame yourself," Malis said. "Draken worked hard to hide his feelings. When that dragon made up his mind, not even the gods could sway him." Her eyes softened. "I'll miss him. He was a good man." She pulled Calista close again and kissed her temple. "And when did your brother decide to throw off his youth?"

So, Calista continued the story. She told how Eon transformed when Draken died and how Solen gave Scratch life with a single touch. How she destroyed entire Ancient fleets with a flick of her hand. Malis beamed with pride at that, but her smile faded when Calista described her final moments with Solen and how she became the fire of Ara.

"Since then, we've been tracking down the Ancients, trying to find their queen." Calista's voice grew quiet, her soul worn thin. "We've picked up more comrades along the way. Champions. Survivors. Fighters." She sighed, defeated. "But still, no queen. We've searched everywhere. It's like she doesn't exist."

"Is that possible?" Malis asked. "Could the Ancients be ruling themselves and only claiming they follow her orders? That's happened before, in other realms."

Calista shook her head slowly. "No. She's out there. I can feel it."

"You can feel it?" Her mother frowned.

"Since bonding with Ara. I can't explain it. I just... know." She gave a weak smile. "I sound crazy, huh?"

"You sound awakened," Malis replied, grasping her hands. "Don't dismiss your intuition, it's a strength, not a flaw." She kissed her daughter's forehead. "Now, let's go see your grandparents. Time to share what's happened and bring everyone up to speed."

Calista nodded, following her mother. Talking had helped, she felt lighter. But her body still buzzed with numb exhaustion, and the rage hadn't faded. Not even Ares had stirred such relentless fury in her as she felt now. Vengeance burned in her veins.

Atlantis hadn't changed much. A few unfamiliar faces passed by as they neared her grandparents' temple. She glanced up at her own temple with a dull ache in her chest. She had once imagined returning home with Solen, showing him where they'd live. Now she'd be alone in that vast bed, overlooking a city she no longer recognized as her own.

The grand temple doors opened, revealing family, crew, and other Atlanteans gathered within.

"Calista!" Shaylane rushed up with a radiant smile, wrapping her in a hug. "We missed you."

Calista returned the embrace, but there was no smile in her. Shaylane stepped back, her own smile softening into sympathy. "Rikar and Kaine told us what happened. I'm so sorry."

There it was, the pity she'd fled from all those years in space. When Rikar first suggested returning to Earth, she'd fought him, insisting they hadn't exhausted every lead. That bought them two more years of searching. Two more years of fighting and two more years of dead ends.

Now she stood beneath the gaze of people who loved her, and all she wanted to do was to disappear.

"Granddaughter." Her grandparents rushed to embrace her. She tried to smile but couldn't.

"It's all right," her grandmother whispered, kissing her cheek. "You don't have to pretend. We're here."

"Thank you, Grandmother," Calista murmured, turning to greet the others. She accepted their condolences and hugs, each one a quiet punch to her gut. She understood their love. She was thankful for it. They meant well, but with each heartfelt expression of sympathy, she wished they had never come home.

"That's pretty." Rowena stepped forward and touched the pendant containing the sands of Ara. As her finger brushed the glass, her eyes widened, her mouth falling open.

"Rowena?" Calista asked. "You okay?"

Rowena pulled back, still staring. Before Calista could ask more, a scream rang through the room.

"You!" A blonde woman charged through the archway, her cheeks streaked with tears, her finger pointed like a dagger. "This is all your fault!"

Power arced from her body, wild and unstable. Calista recognized that chaos; it mirrored her own once.

"Kimi, this isn't her fault," Rikar called, rushing in with Eon behind him. Kimi, Draken's wife and the mother of his child.

"Stop defending her!" Kimi shouted. "Just like your brother, always making excuses for her. She strung him along, and he died because of it! She's anything but innocent. She is the reason your brother left and threw himself to his death. He would do anything for HER!" A bolt of energy burst from her fingertip. Calista didn't move. The energy disintegrated before it reached her.

Kimi snarled. Maybe it was Calista's stillness. Maybe it was the futility. Either way, Kimi screamed and charged, her body lit with fury. Calista could see Kimi's power emanating from her, a power that to others might look intimidating, but to Calista it resembled nothing more than a tiny spark. She could see the others stare in shock at what they were witnessing, but it wasn't Kimi they were looking at; it was Calista.

Calista didn't flinch. The room slowed, the world narrowing to the hurtling storm of Kimi's grief. The phoenix on Calista's back erupted into a spectral flame, wings unfurling wide. She could feel the reluctance from the dragon that usually accompanied the phoenix in her battles, she didn't push him, she understood. She also didn't want Kimi to see him, she didn't hate the woman, but she was done being everyone's punching bag.

She lost a man who had been like a brother to her, only to find out that he felt much more than that for her. Then she lost the man she loved and had to send him to his eternal sleep. She had had enough.

Just as the phoenix was about to descend on Kimi, time halted. Kimi froze mid-lunge. Rikar and Livinia froze mid-intercept. Family, friends; everyone as still as statues.

Then, like a scene rewinding, the moment rolled backward. The phoenix returned to its place on her back. Kimi stood once again at the entrance, now glaring at Eon.

"How could you take her side?" she hissed. "Draken was your hero, you looked up to him."

"He's still my hero," Eon said calmly. "His death doesn't change that."

"Then why stop me?"

"I stopped you to save you." His voice was quiet steel. "Because if Calista fought back, you wouldn't survive. Calton's already lost his father. I didn't want him to lose his mother too."

Kimi's face twisted. "You're saying I can't beat her?"

"I'm saying it wouldn't be a fight. My sister isn't at fault for Draken's death, you need to accept that and move on. If you choose to attack my sister again, I'll not intervene and she'll destroy you. Do you truly want Calton to be left with no one?" He turned and walked away.

Kimi's eyes filled with tears. She glared at Calista. "I won't forget this." She shimmered from the room, leaving a flicker of electric static behind.

Calista stared at the sparks as they faded.

"Calista, it's not your fault," Malis said gently, laying a hand on her shoulder. "You know that, don't you?"

Calista didn't answer. She looked at the faces surrounding her; so full of concern, love, pity. She didn't want their pity. She wanted justice. "I need some time," she whispered. The words trembled in the air.

Before anyone could speak, she shimmered away.

CHAPTER 3

Calista moved along the trail that narrowed as the forest deepened. Moss clung to the stones like ancient green velvet while a chorus of unseen birds echoed from the ravine walls. Their calls overlapped with the distant whisper of falling water. With each step, the sound of the stream grew louder. First a burble, then a steady rush followed by a rhythmic thrum of something stronger. The air turned cool and damp, scented with wet earth and crushed wild mint.

She rounded a bend where the trees parted just enough to reveal the waterfall. It wasn't vast, but it was alive. She moved forward watching the sliver ribbons of water tumbling down dark, polished stones into a glassy pool at the bottom. She smiled watching dragonflies hover over the surface of the pool, their wings glinting like shards of light. A frog plopped into the water with a soft splash. Somewhere above, a goat's bleat echoed faintly from the rocks, but far enough away that she had no worries of any mortals stumbling upon her sanctuary that she found.

Calista had left Atlantis, needing peace and quiet. Here on the island of Samothrace, where the population was fewer than three thousand, she could find a place barely touched by man. The waterfall, nature around her, and the seclusion calmed her soul. Removing her boots, she slowly moved forward into the pool, enjoying the feel of the cool water on her bare feet. She closed her eyes and leaned her head back.

"Hello, granddaughter."

Her eyes opened, and she turned to see Zeus standing there on one of the many rocks that surrounded the pool where she stood.

"Zeus." She acknowledged his presence, though she didn't move. Scratch reached out with one of his hairy legs to move her hair from his way. He wanted to see the Greek God, as well.

Zeus smiled when he saw Scratch. "I see you discovered a cure for your little friend."

She swallowed hard and gave a shake of her head, but said nothing.

Zeus frowned at her. "You didn't?" He gave Scratch a pointed look.

"No, I didn't," she told him, but didn't further explain, her throat tight.

Whether it was the fact that he sensed her pain and didn't push for more of an explanation, or that he didn't care to waste the effort to find out, she wasn't sure. She was glad that rather than press, he just continued, "it doesn't matter how it happened, I'm just glad to see him back where he belongs."

Calista nodded. "Thank you, grandfather." After the battle in Atlantis, when Zeus and the other Greek Gods joined them in their battle against the Ancients, she had forgiven him for his slights against her during her time living with Ares as a father. He wasn't her grandfather, but she still called him that, since that day.

Zeus looked around them, as if taking in the beauty. "You have chosen one of the best places in our land to find refuge."

Calista lifted a shoulder. "I wanted to be alone; this is one of the few places in Greece where you could find some peace."

Zeus nodded. "Tourism has taken over much of this world, and with it came noise, greed, and blind hunger for more. The mortals worship their machines that choke their skies, and their sacred need for a photograph. The Earth groans beneath their weight, and still, they don't listen."

"The mortals have made mistakes." Calista and Zeus turned to see Nyx standing in the shadows of the trees. Calista looked at Zeus, whose eyes widened slightly at seeing the primordial goddess of the night before them. Calista knew that Nyx rarely showed herself to many, though Calista had spoken with her briefly before. Nyx held such power that even Zeus knew to treat her with respect.

Nyx moved forward, from the shadows and into the sun. Her dark hair flowed around her, and her crescent moon staff was held loosely in her hand. Even though she stood in direct sunlight, the sun didn't seem to touch her. All around her, shadows fell as she continued speaking. "But not all of them worship machines. Some of them build with them, heal with them, and even search for answers with them. Some are trying to connect a broken world, not break it further. Tourism isn't just greed; it's also curiosity. It's a longing to feel something ancient, to understand what came before."

"The world is crowded, the mortals are loud and often blind, but they're also learning, fighting, and hoping. This world is no longer perfect; it never was, but it's the only one they have. Most of them are just trying to live without losing themselves completely." Nyx turned to look directly at Zeus, who stayed silent while she spoke. "Hello, Zeus."

"Nyx." Zeus nodded to her. "What brings you here?"

Nyx gave a slight nod in Calista's direction. "I would like a word with our Atlantean princess." Zeus watched Nyx silently. "Alone." Zeus raised both brows before giving a nod to Nyx, then turned to Calista and disappeared with a crack.

Calista turned to watch Nyx silently, unsure of what the goddess wanted with her. When Nyx said nothing for several minutes, Calista could stand the silence no more. "What do you want to talk to me about?" Calista finally asked her.

Nyx moved closer until she stood on the stones around the pool's edge. There she stopped. "I believe it is you, who wants to talk to me."

Calista opened her mouth to respond, but nothing came out. She closed her mouth with a frown. "I'm confused," she admitted.

Nyx watched her though her expression didn't change. "According to the myth the humans like to tell, I'm considered a sister of Gaia, I would figure that you would have questions for me."

"Why would I care about Gaia?" Calista asked, still feeling confused.

Nyx turned away and looked at the trees around them. "I didn't say that you cared about Gaia, not many do. All that live on this planet are her children but yet hardly any even remember who she even is, and they definitely don't believe in her." She turned to look at Calista and said, "not anymore."

Calista's mind wandered back to the night on Ara when Grint told them the story of the Empyreans. Nyx's words echoed what Grint said about Gaia and her children who no longer followed her. "Can Gaia help me find the Ancient's queen?" she asked, then backed up when Nyx turned her dark eyes upon her.

"Now you care about her?" Nyx asked her.

Calista had come into her power, she feared very few, but she wasn't foolish enough to push her luck when she didn't have to. She lowered her gaze, accepting the truth of Nyx's words.

Nyx stood there, waited until Calista raised her head after a few moments, then nodded in satisfaction. "Gaia chose to back away and allow her children to live their own lives, make their own mistakes, and accomplishments. While many believed her gone or sleeping, they couldn't be more wrong."

Calista straightened at Nyx's words, the queen has long been out of her reach, could the game of cat and mouse be coming to an end soon? "Can I speak with her?" she asked, keeping herself contained though she felt a spark of eagerness she hadn't felt in a long time.

"Gaia has sent me to deliver a message."

"Gaia could've chosen anyone to send me a message." Calista spoke watching Nyx closely, she didn't want to anger the goddess, but something wasn't sitting right with her. "Why would she choose someone as powerful as you, to deliver me a message?"

"Would you believe the messenger if they had been a mere mortal, or some minor goddess?" Nyx asked her.

Calista's tongue ran along her suddenly dry lips as she nodded, Nyx was right. She would've believed it to be a trick played by someone working for Ares or one of his minions. "And what is the message?" she asked.

Nyx's eyes narrowed, catching some distant glimmer beyond the trees as though reading a message in the shadows themselves. "Gaia does not grant audience lightly," the goddess said at last, her voice like dusk settling over a still field. "If you would seek her, you must first seek one who still remembers how to kneel in soil and speak her name without fear."

Calista tilted her head. "Who?"

Nyx didn't answer immediately. Instead, she reached down and dipped her fingertips into the black waters of the pool, watching the ripples shift into vague shapes, none of which Calista could fully decipher.

"This person wears no crown, holds no title," Nyx murmured. "They serve drinks to the unworthy and listen more than they speak."

Calista blinked as she mulled Nyx's words over. "They're a bartender?"

Nyx didn't confirm it, but the silence that followed felt heavy with meaning. "I believe this person is with an old friend of yours."

Calista frowned, trying to think of what friend she could be talking about.

"My sister does not believe you are ready," Nyx added. "But the path remains, if you choose to take it. Go to her. If she finds you worthy, she will open the way."

Calista opened her mouth to press for more, but the look in Nyx's eyes silenced her. They shined with starlight now, distant and ancient, far older than the world around them. Nyx rose to her full height, the shadows curling at her feet like obedient mist. Her gaze softened, not with warmth, but with knowing.

"Paths chosen in haste often lead to stone. But those chosen in stillness... may yet bloom." She took one step back. The pool behind her darkened until it became black as night, reflecting no stars.

"Be wary of what you seek, Calista. Gaia listens through root and river, but speaks only to those who remember how to listen back."

With that, her form unraveled into smoke and starlight, the very air folding around the space she'd occupied. In the silence that followed, even the wind seemed to hold its breath. With Nyx gone, the world around Calista brightened again.

Calista stared at the pool where Nyx had stood, her reflection now the only thing staring back. She sighed and moved out of the pool, her intent to head back to Atlantis to let the others know her plans, when a movement stopped her.

She turned to see Zeus standing there and frowned. "Eavesdropping?"

Zeus snorted. "Not even I am brave enough to risk the wrath of Nyx out of mild curiosity."

"So, why are you here?" she asked.

"I knew when she left and wanted to impart some of my own wisdom before you rush off to this adventure of yours," he told her, and chuckled at her raised brow. "Yes, granddaughter, I do have some wise words left in me. You can decide if they are worth listening to."

Calista paused then shrugged a shoulder. "Sure, why

not? It's not like I have an abundance of advice or instructions on what to do."

"Don't give in to the rage," he told her, to which she frowned at him.

"What do you mean?" she asked him.

"All that rage you have pent up within you, use it if you must, but be careful to not let it consume you," he told her and breathed in deeply. "It will only harm you in your quest, will only bring you heartache. That rage is the same I saw in my son, Ares, so long ago. I never tried to help him with that rage, instead I watched as it consumed him. I don't want to make the same mistake with you, and I don't want you to go down the same road."

Calista frowned, but before she could speak, Zeus vanished in a flash of light. The crack of his lightning bolt echoed around her, and she flinched. When she looked again, he was gone.

"I'm not Ares!" she spoke between gritted teeth to the empty air around her.

Chapter 4

I'm nothing like Ares!" Calista roared, hurling an energy sphere with all her fury.

The blast struck the nearest statue which ended up being Brax. It splintered the head from the body with a thunderous crack. Stone splinters sprayed the marble floor as the decapitated head rolled several feet, finally thudding to a stop in front of another monument.

She turned on her heel, teeth clenched, breath ragged. Her hands still crackled with lingering power. She looked around the garden outside her grandparent's temple. She had come home after her talk with Zeus, but didn't want to see anyone until she felt calmer.

A familiar voice cut through the echo. "I have to admit... definite improvement on Brax's statue."

Calista spun to find her father, Cael, casually holding the severed stone head. The sculpted face of Brax still wore that self-important smirk. Atmos's acolytes had done their job too well.

"I always said it didn't capture his true essence," Cael said, tossing the head over his shoulder without ceremony. It clattered out of sight.

A reluctant smile tugged at Calista's lips.

"Who had the gall to tell you you're like Ares?" he asked, approaching.

"Zeus," she muttered, folding her arms.

Cael stopped, his expression tightening. He stepped forward and pulled her into a firm, protective hug.

"And you're listening to a Greek? Since when did we start trusting them for emotional insight?"

She gave a soft, choked laugh and let herself melt into his embrace. "I missed you, dad."

"I missed you too, kiddo," he said, brushing his lips across her hair. "It's good to have you home."

Calista stayed quiet, still leaning against him. The silence lingered long enough that he gently asked, "what exactly did Zeus say?"

Reluctantly, she pulled back and walked over to a stone bench. Her fingers wrapped around the back like she needed grounding.

"He said I've got... pent-up rage. That I need to deal with it before I see Gaia. That if I don't, it'll consume me like it did Ares."

Cael folded his arms and studied her. "Do you think he's wrong?"

She turned to face him, frustrated. "I don't have time for rage, dad. I have a war to fight. Friends to honor. A queen to find. Rage doesn't help me; it just gets in the way."

He raised a brow and looked over her shoulder, toward the shattered remains of Brax's likeness.

"That doesn't count," she said quickly, glaring at the ruined statue. "Even Rowena wanted to knock his smug head off."

Cael laughed. "True. But she showed restraint. You, on the other hand..."

Calista groaned and dropped her head into her hands. "I'm not Ares. I swear I'm not."

"No," Cael said softly, walking over. "You're better than he ever was. You carry love, grief, fire, hope. But even the strongest of us bleed when we're cut. And you, Calista, have been wounded; over and over."

She didn't respond, just let herself lean into his side when he wrapped an arm around her.

"Don't be afraid of your rage," he said gently. "Just... don't let it decide who you become."

Calista closed her eyes. For a brief, fleeting moment, she let the battle slip from her shoulders and just be a daughter; safe in the arms of someone who remembered who she was before the war began.

"One who still remembers how to kneel in soil and speak her name without fear?" Rowena repeated softly, her brow creased in thought.

Calista watched her from nearby, arms crossed, pacing slightly as the weight of Nyx's message gnawed at her. After talking with her father, they both entered her grandparent's temple, to tell everyone what Nyx had said.

Kaine leaned against a stone pillar, watching her with quiet concern. Rikar stood with Livinia near one of the crystal sconces, their fingers barely touching, a silent show of solidarity between them.

"Does Gaia still have acolytes?" Tylaos asked, glancing toward Rowena, who held a softly glowing crystal orb in one hand. Her fingers traced slow, thoughtful circles across its surface, as though stroking the memory of something long forgotten.

Atmos leaned casually against the wall, a lump of clay in his hands that was already beginning to take shape beneath his skilled fingers. As the others spoke, he molded it without looking, until the form of a raven emerged. With a final pass of his thumb, he held it up briefly in the light before clapping his hands together. A dull squish sounded, and when he opened them again, a sleek black raven with glinting eyes blinked up at him.

With a single squawk, it launched into the air, beating its wings once before flying out through the open window.

"Our acolytes are still with us," Atmos said, flashing Calista a wink. She stared after the raven, unsure if it was meant to be an answer or a trick.

She turned back to see the others nodding. Salis, thoughtful as always, had a piece of wheat between his teeth, chewing absently as he stared off in contemplation.

"We have some acolytes who stayed beneath the waves with us," he said slowly, "rather than be seduced by the new world above." His voice took on a somber weight. "But the Greeks, most of them abandoned their deities long ago. Who could blame them? Their gods toyed with them like pieces on a game board. It's no wonder faith gave way to folklore." He gave a short shake of his head. "I'd be surprised if anyone still remembers Gaia beyond the pages of dusty myths."

"Still," Lison countered, resting her chin on her palm, "someone had to keep the stories alive. Even if they're written as myths, doesn't that mean that someone still believes?" She shrugged lightly; her hands dropped to her side. "Stories fade when no one cares to tell them."

"Not necessarily..." came Shaylane's soft voice as she entered the temple. Her father, Brax, followed with a familiar scowl carved deep into his features. Calista bit her lip and dropped her gaze, rather than look into Brax's.

Shaylane stepped forward, voice low and measured, either not noticing Calista's reaction to her father or just not acknowledging it. "Just because something is written doesn't mean it's believed. People write what sells. Some would put anything on a page, true or not, if it fills their coffers."

Calista let out a sigh and tilted her head back to stare at the ceiling. "So, what I'm hearing is, acolytes may exist... or they may not." She waved a hand dismissively. "Super helpful."

A moment of silence passed before Rowena finally

spoke, her voice distant, yet certain. "All gods have acolytes; even in this world. Their numbers may be fewer, and they often worship in secret now. But they're out there. The faithful don't vanish... they adapt."

"So how do we find one of these acolytes?" Calista asked, her voice sharp with urgency. At the raised brow from her mother, she gave Rowena an apologetic look. "I meant no disrespect, I'm just frustrated. We've been looking for the queen for so long and when I finally have a possible lead, that we can't say for sure is a true lead, I don't know where to go."

Rowena nodded in acceptance to her apology and then continued, "We start with Nyx's second clue. She let the crystal dissolve into a shimmering mist. "The person we're looking for serves drinks to the unworthy and listens more than they speak."

"That sounds like a bartender," Calista muttered, rubbing her temple. "But Nyx wouldn't confirm it. Even if I'm right, there are a million bars across the world."

"How many of those bars are run by someone you know?" Kaine asked, tilting his head curiously.

Before Calista could answer, the heavy stone doors creaked open. Eon stepped in, quieter than usual. Since the incident with Kimi, he'd been more withdrawn; less laughter, more silence. She missed his impulsive optimism and goofy humor, but now, every step he took carried purpose. He wasn't a boy anymore. Allen and John followed him, talking excitedly to one another about all that they've seen in Atlantis.

"We're heading to Las Vegas," he said, his voice even. "Anyone want to come?"

"Las Vegas?" her mother repeated slowly, the name unfamiliar on her tongue.

Calista gave a wry smile then took a deep breath as she tried to find the right way to describe an entire city built on neon lights and sleepless sin to someone who'd never left Atlantis, much less stepped foot in the mortal realm

"It's called the city that never sleeps," Eon offered. "A good place for someone restless to disappear for a while."

Calista gave him a grateful glance. "Exactly. One night, I couldn't sleep and just... wandered. I stumbled into this bar hidden behind a bookcase in a casino. That's where I met a bartender named John Stahle."

Rikar and Livinia exchanged a glance. "Wasn't that the bartender who gave you some strange drink?" Rikar asked.

"Yeah," Calista nodded with a smirk. "He even named it after himself, called it a 'John Stahle.'"

"No ego there," Livinia noted.

Her father raised a brow at her words and remarked, "this coming from someone who claims they are the best assassin in all the worlds?" Her father wasn't happy when he learned that Livinia had kidnapped her and

Rikar, to deliver them to the Ancients. Even though they assured him that she did help in their escape, he still acted leery around her. When he pointed out that if she hadn't kidnapped them, that Draken would still be alive, Rikar got in his face and told him to be careful with his words.

Her father had stood his ground against the man he once called his closest friend, and Calista was certain that if it hadn't been for her mother's intervention, the two would've come to blows. The man known for his easy laughter and warm spirit had vanished; replaced by something fierce and unyielding. In that moment, Cael didn't look like the lighthearted man she'd always known. He looked like an avenging angel, forged by fury and driven by the instinct to protect his daughter at all costs.

"Careful, Cael," Rikar said sharply, pushing off the wall with narrowed eyes.

Calista's stomach twisted. She hated this. Hated that they were all turning on each other when they should've been united. Hated that no matter how hard she tried to move forward, the past still bled into the present.

Cael didn't back down. He met Rikar's stare. "What's wrong? I asked a fair question. Are you afraid of her answer?"

Livinia stepped between them, her expression unshaken. Her braids shifted around her shoulders as if echoing her mood. "I can speak for myself," she said, voice steady. "And it's not ego when it's the truth."

Rikar clenched his jaw, but retreated back to the wall. Calista gave her mother a silent plea for help.

Thankfully, Malis stepped in.

"So... are you guys going to this Stahle's then?" she asked, cutting through the tension and turning the conversation back to Calista.

"I doubt that it's still there." Calista wrinkled her nose. "That was so long ago."

"I would like to see this 'Las Vegas' though," Allen said with John nodding his head next to him. "Eon was telling us all about the lights and people dancing in the streets."

"I think we should all go," Cael declared, rising from his seat. "You said there are lots of bars there, maybe we can find the one the acolyte is hiding in."

Malis placed a calming hand on his shoulder, stopping him. "We'll stay here, but stay ready. Just in case."

Cael frowned. "I want to help our daughter."

"You won't help anyone by fighting with your oldest friend," Malis said, her tone gentle but unwavering.

Cael opened his mouth to argue, but Malis's gaze held firm. He let out a long breath and looked at Calista. "You'll call if you need us?"

"Of course I will," she assured him. She stepped forward and hugged them both, feeling steadied by their embrace despite the chaos still bubbling around them.

Just then, a high-pitched chitter echoed through the chamber. A small shape dropped from the rafters and landed lightly on Calista's shoulder. She grinned.

"There you are," she whispered.

Scratch, the spider who had been sealed in a teardrop necklace for most of his life, curled a leg around her hair in greeting. He had disappeared after their return to Atlantis, off exploring the corners of the home he never got to see while imprisoned.

Thanks to Zeus and his intervention, Scratch had survived. And now, as always, he was ready to follow her into whatever danger came next.

"You ready to go?" she asked, smiling slightly at his enthusiastic nod.

She turned to Eon, her eyes determined. "Ready to explore Las Vegas again?"

"I'm going too," Kaine said, stepping forward. "I want to see more of this world... and try that John Stahle drink you mentioned."

"If they still make it." Calista told him.

He shrugged. "If not, I'm sure they will have something good."

Rikar scoffed. "We'll come too. You'll need someone who won't be distracted by flashy lights and fancy drinks."

Calista groaned. Kaine rolled his eyes. Her father narrowed his eyes again, but before anyone said anything, a deep voice cut through.

"Does anyone know what happened to my statue?" Brax asked suspiciously, eyeing both Cael and Calista.

Cael smirked but said nothing.

“Cael can explain,” Malis said quickly, stepping in again. “While they go visit Las Vegas. Let’s not start another argument.”

Calista looked around at the team forming around her: Eon, John, Allen, Kaine, Rikar, Livinia, and Scratch. Her family, by blood or by battle.

She nodded. “To Vegas,” she said. “Let’s go find the one who remembers how to speak Gaia’s name.”

Chapter 5

Calista looked around her to see that it was almost nightfall in Las Vegas. A dazzling display of neon lights with towering hotel casinos glowing in every color, and the constant flicker of digital billboards. There were street performers entertaining the crowds, and the air buzzed with excitement, laughter, and the hum of nightlife that never sleeps.

She turned back to see Eon walk away from them, Rikar and Livinia followed him closely, she rushed to catch up to them.

"Do you know where he is going?" Kaine looked over at Calista.

She shook her head. "Nope, just following."

"This place is pretty damn cool."

Calista turned to see Kaine pulling at John with a shake of his head. "Come on, man. We have to keep up with the kid." John had been enthralled by the street dancers who twirled and jerked to the beat of the music.

John turned away from the lights, his head turned to look at Eon who still walked with a purpose. "Kid? He doesn't look like a kid to me."

Kaine slapped his hand to his forehead. "Trust me, at one point he was a kid."

John's eyes crinkled. "Weren't we all, at one point?"

"Just, let's go!" Kaine shoved John away from the dancers with a grunt. "Man, you can be any size you want, why must you pick this one?"

John shrugged. "I like this size, it fits me."

"Fine, just move," Kaine grumbled as he followed Eon with John ambling behind him. Since joining them, John had taken to Kaine.

Allen followed them, his gaze moving back to the dancers. "Good thing Cellica isn't here, we wouldn't be able to pull her away from them."

Kaine sighed. "Probably not, better for her to stay on the ship with the rest of them."

Calista agreed though she kept her thoughts to herself as they moved up stairs and down outside hallways before Eon entered one of the many buildings in Vegas. They passed shops of trinkets and expensive looking clothing before Eon stopped in front of a bookcase. Calista watched as he hooked his finger on the big red book and pulled.

"Whoa!" Kaine stared as the bookcase swung open, revealing velvet booths, dimly lit lounge, and the bar that looked as if it had frozen in time.

Calista ran her fingers along the wood grain of the wall; her eyes wandered around the bar as she took in all that she saw. It felt as if nothing had changed, even though it had been many decades since she left Earth. She moved slowly around the bar; past the dance floor she had graced many of times. As they reached the bar, Calista still looked around, surprised at how so much had stayed the same.

The clink of glass came first, then the cool press against her skin. She turned to see a glass beside her arm, filled with amber liquid that carried the familiar scent of polished wood and sharp ginger. She looked up, barely containing her shock.

The same black arm garters over the same white sleeves, polishing a glass with the same white cloth. The same twinkle in those eyes that showed no passage of age, even though she had been gone so long.

"John?" She frowned looking at him.

He nodded to her glass; the same friendly expression she remembered staring at her. She lifted the glass to her lips, tasting the warm liquid, bourbon with a touch of ginger. "Still good?" he asked her.

She nodded, but stayed silent.

He smiled and then turned to the others. "You want John Stahle's as well, or would you rather something else?" His brows furrowed when Eon moved closer. "You seem familiar."

Eon shrugged. "I've been around. I'll try a John Stahle."

John nodded. He raised a finger. "John Stahle's all around." He turned back to Calista, who hadn't taken her eyes off of him. "Do I have broccoli between my teeth?" he asked her.

She took a sip of her drink before she answered. "How can this be?" she asked him.

"What?" he asked her while the others watched and listened closely.

"I've been gone for a long time, many decades." She gave a shake of her head. "You look the same as the day I first walked into this bar. You shouldn't be here, you shouldn't look the same, you shouldn't be alive." Rather than react to her words as she expected, he reached for the glasses that another server brought out on a serving tray. He placed them down in front of the others and turned back to Calista, who blurted out, "no human can live that long."

John chuckled. "Who says I'm human?"

"One who serves drinks to the unworthy..." Calista whispered to herself.

"Hmmm?" John tilted his head at her.

"Are you the one Gaia wants me to find?" Calista spoke low while she leaned close to him.

John's smile didn't fade. Instead, he lowered his head so that only she could hear him. "No," he said simply, the word carrying a strange weight. "But the one you seek is closer than you think."

Calista pulled back, her brow furrowed. "Then who?"

John straightened and wiped down a dry spot on the

counter, slow and methodical, before he nodded toward the far end of the room where several empty tables waited in the flickering low light. "Take a seat," he said, setting the cloth aside. "Order nothing. Say nothing. Just...be." He looked at her then, gaze steady. "If you're meant to find them, they'll come."

Before she could ask another question, John was already moving down the bar, whistling a tune she couldn't place; one that made the hairs on her arms stand on end. She turned to the others who stood there, their glasses still full. "I guess we sit." She gestured towards the tables and after a brief pause, they all moved to sit.

Livinia sat down, her gaze watching a group of males sitting at a table several over from them. The males were staring at the screen on a phone. She turned to Rikar and asked him, "what are those males doing?"

He looked over and frowned, "I'm not sure. We were never ones to mingle with mortals much."

Calista peered over at the table to see what was on the screen of their phone. "Looks like they are watching a baseball game." She looked around. "This bar is set back in the era where there were no TVs, so they have to bring their own mini-internet devices to watch any games they choose." She looked over at John Stahle, who was talking to a brunette dressed in the same bartender garb as John. "If John sees them, he'll kick them out. Today's technology isn't really allowed in here, or at least it wasn't when I first came here."

"What is baseball?" Livinia asked.

Rykar leaned back in his seat, staring up at the ceiling and took a deep breath. "Baseball is basically a game where one hits a leather ball with a heavy wooden stick. Then the batter runs around a diamond shaped track to the beginning and then they get points."

"A game?" she asked with a tilt of her head.

"Basically, they learn the game at a young age where they play for fun. When they get older, they start watching it religiously." Calista shrugged.

Livinia looked back over at the males who were starting to get loud, which attracted John's attention who walked over to the table. After a few words were exchanged, they handed over the phone, looking very disappointed.

"Why would anyone worship children's games?"

"No idea." Calista answered and turned her attention back to the dance floor, watching the dancers while they waited for their contact.

Several hours later, they still sat at the tables, their glasses now empty and their gazes on the dancers on the floor. The woman wore knee-length flapper dresses with beaded strands bouncing with their movements. The guys wore loose fitting trousers, suspenders and a crisp button-up shirt with rolled sleeves. The dances they were doing didn't look like anything Calista remembered from the twenties.

Their fingers were outstretched, while their palms

were facing down, looking as if they had claws. Hands would bounce from side to side while they would tap their toes to the music. With each turn they would lower their bodies for several turns and then they would rise back in the same manner.

John was watching a blond moving on the floor, her hands moving while she laughed. He tilted his head as he watched. Calista couldn't blame him; the girl was something to look at.

"The Spider."

Calista turned to see a set of dark eyes looking down at her. "I'm sorry." Calista frowned up at her. "What are you talking about?" Her body stiffened at hearing Solen's nickname for her come from a stranger's lips.

The woman nodded towards the dance floor. "The dance." She shrugged. "It's called the Spider. It's the latest craze."

Calista turned her gaze back to the dance floor, she frowned. "Don't look anything like a spider."

"I don't think so either, but it seems to have taken off with the younger generation." She lifted all the glasses with her fingers and placed them on a tray. "My name is Sav and I'll be serving you tonight."

Calista nodded. "Hello, Sav. I don't suppose you know of anyone that we should be waiting for, do you?"

Sav gave a shrug of her shoulders, "I'm just the server tonight, helping John at the bar and tables. Sorry."

"That's all right." Calista told her.

"You want another John Stahle's, or feeling adventurous tonight?" Sav asked, leaning casually against the table's edge, a playful glint in her eyes.

Calista twirled her finger along the rim of her empty glass, the moisture from the last sip cooling her skin. "Depends. What else do you have?"

Sav straightened with a grin. "We've got something called a Savtastic. It's a punchy blend of tropical fruit juices, smooth rum, and just enough tang to make your lips pucker and your heart skip."

Her gaze drifted over the group, pausing on John, who hadn't said a word. He was still staring at the dance floor like he'd forgotten they were in a speakeasy-inspired lounge and not a dream. Then her eyes flicked back to Calista.

"I'll try it," Calista said with a small smile. Around the table, the others nodded in agreement; everyone except John, who remained glued to whatever held his attention in the crowd.

Kaine let out a long, exaggerated sigh and elbowed him; hard.

John blinked and glanced down at him, a frown tugging at his lips. "Wha?"

"She asked if you want to try a Savtastic," Kaine muttered, clearly annoyed.

John's eyes lifted to Calista, then slid right back to the dance floor. "Will that get me a date with the pretty little blonde out there?"

Sav stared at him before she asked him, "you want me to get you a date with my girlfriend?"

"Yeah." John nodded, his eyes still on the dance floor, oblivious to the looks he was getting from everyone at the table.

"John," Kaine growled at him.

Sav turned to Calista and held out a card to her, before she could apologize for John's apparent insensitivity and clueless manner. "What's this?" Calista asked her.

"You want to see Gaia, follow those directions. They'll take you to one who can help you find her." Sav told her.

"You're not the one we've been sent to see?" Calista asked, turning the card over in her hands, feeling some aggravation simmer within her. The card was blank; nothing was on it. She wasn't in the mood for riddles and games. Why couldn't someone just be straight with her, tell her how to rid the galaxies of the Ancients and their queen.

"Oh, I am." Sav told her, snapping her from her aggravation to stare up at Sav with confusion.

"Then what is this?" Calista asked, holding up the card.

Sav said nothing but moved over to the dancefloor where the blond moved into her arms with a smile. Sav turned around, not even sparing John a glance, and told Calista, "seek out Alvia, the card will tell you where to find him, maybe he can show you the way."

Calista looked back down at the card, as she watched, words started to appear. She looked up to say something to Sav, but Sav was gone and so was the blond. She released a sigh.

"Way to go, John." Kaine cuffed John upside his head in frustration.

"Hey! How was I supposed to know?" John mumbled, looking down. "I just thought she was pretty."

Calista looked down at the card and read the words, her brow furrowing. Great, another quest.

She felt a hand grip the back of her chair; she looked up to see John Stahle look at them. "Who upset Sav?"

The whole table pointed to John who gave a big sigh, his shoulders drooping.

John Stahle gave a laugh and then shook his head. "You might not want him to join you on your adventure." He turned to leave, but stopped when Calista touched his arm. He turned to her. "Yes?"

"How do you know that Sav is sending us on an adventure?" she asked him.

"Because, that is what I would do if you had upset me," he told her, then gave a wink before disappearing back behind his bar.

"He's right," Kaine said looking at John who hung his head. "You need to stay back, buddy. I'm sorry."

Allen moved next to John, placed his hand on the big guy's shoulder. "That's all right John, I'll stay with you. We can go visit with Bastion and Cellica back on the ship. I bet Bastion has made some of that fruity desert you like." John looked up at him with a big grin. "Much better than getting frustrated over another riddle."

Calista turned to Eon. "You should go back with them," she suggested.

Eon didn't budge, just stared back at his sister. "I'm not staying behind. Where you go, I go. I'm in this with you, sis."

Calista sighed but nodded. A part of her wanted to argue with him but another part understood.

CHAPTER 6

So, how do we find this Alvia?" Rikar asked as they left Stahle's, the lights of Las Vegas glowing brightly around them.

Calista looked down at the card in her hand, looking at the key that was taped to it, and then turned it over to read the writing. "Your room isn't the destination, look lower. Take the lift, press PB, and don't look back." She looked back up and lifted her shoulders. "I'm not sure what that means."

Kaine held up his hands. "Don't look at me, I know practically nothing about this world."

Calista, Eon, and Rikar frowned at one another. Calista flicked the card in her hand, chewing on her bottom lip.

"Take the lift..." Eon murmured with a frown. "Lift what?"

"That don't sound right." Rikar gave a shake of his head.

"You do know another name for a lift is an elevator, right?"

They turned around to see John Stahle watching them with a grin.

Calista frowned at him. "Are you following us?"

He tilted his head to look at her. "You're in my town and asking me if I'm following you?" Calista crossed her arms and stared back at him, her lips pressed together. After a moment, he chuckled. "I'm not following you, actually, I'm going to meet a friend. I told you about him, it's been a while, but during one of your visits, I told you about him."

Calista arched a brow but said nothing. Instead, she lifted both hands, palms up, and a slight shrug in her shoulders. Her expression didn't shift, but the challenge in her eyes stayed sharp.

John grinned. "We went to Mexico for work and got stuck in the elevator together. Took us almost half an hour before we realized that the peanut butter button actually meant ground floor in Mexico." He winked at her, waved to the others before he turned and walked away.

"What was that all about?" Kaine looked at Calista who stood there, staring straight ahead with her mouth slack. "Calista?"

She closed her mouth and turned back to others. "I know where we need to go."

Rikar looked at her then towards where John Stahle disappeared to, then back to Calista. "From what he said?"

She nodded. "I know it sounds silly, but the story he is talking about happened in Mexico where they were stuck in an elevator at a hotel. There was a button labeled PB, his friend made a joke about someone bringing them a peanut butter sandwich if they pushed it. They found out it actually meant planta baja, which means ground floor in Mexico."

"Do you know what hotel?" Eon asked her but she shook her head.

"No, but it's still better than what we had when we left the bar," she said with a sigh.

"Well, then let's go find a hotel," Kaine said. Calista nodded and looked at Eon who created one of his swirling vortexes for them to walk through.

John Stahle stood there and watched them disappear through the vortex, his lips twitching. "You got something to say?"

"You're just trying to piss me off, aren't you?" Sav glared at John.

"I don't have any idea what you mean." His lips still twitched.

"That is the last time I use a story of yours to teach someone a lesson." She turned away from him and stalked away.

His lips pulled into a grin as he watched her walk away.

"We keep getting weird looks." Kaine noticed when they walked out of the latest hotel, where they walked in right past the front desk to the elevators, and there they hit the PB button as soon as the doors shut but it only opened right back up at the main floor.

"Trust me, this isn't the weirdest thing those people have seen." Calista assured him.

"As long as they don't give us any problems," Kaine said as they moved out into the bright sunlight. Moving past the tall stone walls with barbed wire along the tops.

"If you're scared, Eon can always send you back to the ship with John and Allen," Rikar told him as he walked ahead of them into the next hotel.

Kaine raised a brow and looked at Calista who just shook her head. "Let's just get this done and over with," she spoke with a tired voice as they entered yet another hotel. Calista sighed as they entered yet another elevator. She jabbed the PB button, ignoring Rikar's movement to press it, as well as his raised brow.

She crossed her arms and waited for the doors to open at the main floor once again. When the doors didn't open her back straightened. She looked around and saw the others straighten as well, except for Livinia whose posture was always rigid. When her gaze moved over to her brother, he was staring straight ahead at the elevator doors. Since Draken's death, she couldn't name one time when he joked around or even smiled.

Her gaze moved to the doors, wondering what they would see when the doors opened. Her eyes moved to above the doors where instead of numbers counting down like in most elevators, multi-colored lights were swirling in a ball. When the swirling stopped and the lights dimmed, they could feel the lift slowing down until it stopped with a jerk. Her stomach clenched as she waited for the doors to open.

With a ping, the doors opened.

"Wow!" Kaine breathed as he took in the view in front of them. "Bastion would love this."

Calista nodded at his words and stepped off the elevator, the others trailing behind, though none could look away from what waited beyond the open doors. Where they expected a basement or sterile hallway, an immense forest stretched in every direction, lush and alive with ancient magic. The air hummed with quiet energy, thick with the scent of damp earth, blooming nectar, and something older… something sacred.

Earthen paths wound through groves of towering trees, their trunks smooth as marble, their bark veined with soft light that pulsed like a heartbeat. Some leaves spread wider than sails, hanging like natural canopies, their undersides glistening with dew that shimmered in the glow of floating orbs suspended in midair. These orbs drifted lazily above the paths, casting a soft golden light that seemed to respond to movement, brightening slightly as they approached.

Bushes heavy with multicolored blossoms lined the trail, their petals shifting hues as though reacting to emotion or thought. Flowers turned subtly toward the group as they passed, their stamens quivering, curious. Overhead, birds with iridescent wings and trailing tails sang in layered harmonies, weaving through branches like living music. Somewhere in the distance, water trickled gently, accompanied by the faint chime of bells that didn't seem to come from any visible source.

The forest was impossibly vast, yet it wrapped around them with the quiet intimacy of something watching. Alive. Aware.

Even the enchanted wilds of the Aggies back on Ara seemed pale in comparison, this wasn't just nature. This was a place that breathed.

Rikar reached toward a nearby bush, its blossoms shaped like coiled dragons mid-roar. He brushed his fingers around the stem of a deep violet bloom when a sudden, guttural grunt echoed through the trees.

"I wouldn't pluck any of my flowers," a raspy voice warned from the shadows, "not if you're hoping for my help getting an audience with Gaia."

The group jerked to attention, spinning toward the sound. From a narrow, shadow-draped path between the trees, a figure shuffled forward. At first glance, it appeared short and squat, but as it drew closer, they saw the truth; not small, just hunched.

A tangled curtain of silver hair veiled the figure's face, but as he lifted his head, the strands parted to reveal an elderly man. His skin looked like bark; weathered and creased. His smile showed hollows where teeth had once been. Long white hair dragged across the earthen path behind him, swaying in rhythm with each step.

He leaned heavily on a wooden staff; its gnarled surface wrapped in ivy. At its top sat a glass bauble, swirling with liquid color; shimmering blues, greens, and golds shifting like trapped starlight. His cloak appeared grown rather than sewn, a living tapestry of bark, vine, and leaf that trailed behind him, rustling softly with each step.

Growing directly from the hunch on his back was a small, crooked tree; its thin trunk rising just over his head. A single branch jutted sideways, and from it hung a sleeping bat, wings curled in like folded parchment. At the base of the limb, a slender pine marten lay coiled, its bushy tail tucked beneath its chin like a pillow. The branch swung gently as the man walked, but neither creature stirred.

With every step he took, the earth beneath him responded; grass sprouting fresh, tiny wildflowers blooming in his wake, as though the forest itself recognized him.

"Are you Alvia?" Calista asked, stepping forward.

The hunched figure tilted his head, peering up at her with one sharp, unimpressed eye. "No," he said dryly. "I'm the emperor of the moon and part-time mariachi dancer. Of course I'm Alvia."

He rolled his eyes with theatrical exaggeration before turning away, muttering just loud enough for them all to hear. "You travel across worlds, take an elevator into an enchanted forest, clearly nowhere near the basement, and still ask if I'm Alvia. Remarkable. Absolutely dazzling levels of perception."

Calista's cheeks flushed. "No need to be rude," she said, her voice steady, though she kept her tone restrained. She didn't know what kind of power he held, and they needed him, whether she liked it or not.

Alvia turned back to her, expression pinched in mock concern. "Rude? Darling, if that bruised your ego, I'd rethink this whole quest. You're not climbing a staircase here, you're plunging into chaos, and manners aren't going to be your shield."

Behind her, Rikar growled low, his voice vibrating with the unmistakable edge of a dragon. His eyes glinted, turning dragon-like, though he stayed human. Thankfully.

Alvia didn't flinch. He didn't even blink. If anything, he looked slightly amused.

Calista straightened, her chin lifting. "I lived under Ares for centuries. I can handle anything you throw at me."

Alvia snorted. "Really? And when exactly was this grand age of survival?"

She blinked. "What?"

He gave an exasperated sigh, rubbing the bridge of his nose as though she were the one inconveniencing him. "How long ago was that, princess? When you were under Ares? Because if you're drawing courage from faded glories, you might want to update your armor."

Calista inhaled slowly. "Thousands of years ago, yes, but some scars don't fade, and neither does the strength that forged them. I can handle this."

Alvia didn't respond at first, just gave a skeptical grunt. "We'll see," he muttered, turning again and trudging down the path. His hunch swayed slightly with each step, the tree sprouting from his back bobbing along. Neither the bat nor the marten stirred.

Kaine glanced at the others, hesitant. "Should we… follow him?"

Calista said nothing. She wasn't sure anymore. None of this made sense. Rikar and Livinia kept their eyes on the old man, their expressions unreadable. Eon tilted his head, studying Alvia like he was decoding a riddle.

Alvia didn't bother turning around. His voice drifted back to them, high-pitched and dripping with mockery. "Hmm… should we follow the only being who can lead us to Gaia? Or should we stand here, blinking like confused tourists while he vanishes into the forest?"

His walking stick thumped harder into the earth. "So many questions. So little common sense."

He kept walking. After a heartbeat, the others exchanged looks before they followed.

Livinia took the lead, her eyes narrowed, never leaving Alvia's swaying back.

Chapter 7

The distant roar of rushing water grew louder with each step as they trailed behind Alvia. The soft dirt beneath their feet gradually gave way to uneven stone, slick with moisture and speckled with moss. The air thickened with the scent of fresh water, damp earth, and the faint, ancient perfume of moss-covered bark. As they rounded a bend, the trees parted to reveal a hidden oasis. A waterfall cascading down a wall of dark stone, spilling into a crystalline pool that shimmered in the dappled light. Lush ferns and flowering vines framed the scene, their colors vivid against the silver spray.

For a breathless moment, Calista was transported as if she were once again on Samothrace, surrounded by untamed beauty. Ahead, Alvia stepped confidently onto a stone path that wound around the edge of the pool and disappeared behind the curtain of falling water.

"A waterfall." Eon frowned as he looked around them.

"Truly, your powers of observation rival the Oracles of old," Alvia murmured, casting a sidelong glance. "Do warn us if the sun dares rise next."

Calista frowned at Alvia who kept moving towards the waterfall, who was this sarcastic little man with his sharp tongue? She was truly trying to keep her thoughts to herself, the fact that they needed him to find Gaia, kept her silent. Though, his manner was enough to make the most patient aggravated. She doubted even Vapor, the Atlantean goddess of calm and tranquility, would be able to stay calm with him.

"Why are we here?" Livinia asked as she moved next to Calista, her eyes on Alvia.

Alvia didn't pause in his back-and-forth ambling, the tree branch swaying. "You want an audience with Gaia?" he asked, his gruff voice showing his agitation.

Livinia's eyes widened and her lips tightened. "Of course," she answered.

"Then quit asking questions and follow me." He motioned towards the waterfall, that he was only feet from, with the walking staff. The bauble glinted on top of the staff. "There's a cave behind the waterfall, enter there and if you make it out, then we can continue our journey."

"And if we don't?" Rikar asked, he moved to stand next to Livinia, his dark gaze watching Alvia.

"Not my problem," Alvia told him as he ambled under the waterfall and disappeared.

Livinia gave a nonchalant shrug before stepping forward, her silhouette swallowed by the shimmering curtain of falling water. A fine mist clung to the air, dampening hair and lashes as the others followed in her wake, one by one, moving cautiously along the narrow stone pathway. Each step was deliberate, their feet slick against the moss-covered stones, the roar of the waterfall a constant thunder in their ears. Cold sprays kissed their faces, sharp and sudden like the breath of the mountain itself. The stone wall behind the cascade loomed close, worn smooth and glistening like glass from centuries of relentless water carving its mark. The path curved gently inward, pulling them deeper beneath the cascade's veil, into the waiting hush beyond.

The farther they ventured, the deeper the darkness grew, swallowing the light bit by bit. Shadows thickened like fog, pressing in on all sides until the path ahead vanished entirely. Their steps slowed to cautious shuffles, arms outstretched, fingers brushing against damp stone as their eyes strained to pierce the gloom. Within moments, even the space just inches in front of them dissolved into black.

"Hey, Rikar," Kaine called out. "You're half-dragon, can you create some fire to light the way?" Kaine asked as he inched along the murky darkness, his steps tentative while he felt along the stone walls. He paused when there was no response, not even the growl that he expected. "Rikar?"

Still no response.

"Calista?"

Nothing.

"Anyone?" As soon as those words left his lips the world around him brightened, so much that he had to raise his hand to shield his eyes. When he lowered his hand, his mouth went agape at what he saw before him. He was home, back on Ara, but no longer was the land dry and dead the way it was when they left the planet. There were colors and flora all around.

"Come on, man!"

Kaine turned to see Solen standing there grinning at him, his hands on his hips. This wasn't the Solen who died on Ara, this was the Solan from his youth. Before his best friend became the great Hunter of Ara. When he moved forward, he realized that it wasn't just Solen who had gone back in time. He no longer stood over six feet tall; he was lucky if he stood past four feet.

"Come on, we need to get to Sala Way before the ceremony is over." Solen looked back to his friend, motioning for him to follow.

"Ceremony?" Kaine started after his friend, his speed faster in his youth.

Solen frowned at him. "The Rites, remember?"

"Oh, yeah," Kaine said, then flinched when Solen punched his shoulder, like they both had done to each other so much in their youth.

"Let's go, I don't want to miss it." Solen grinned as he jumped from stone to a fallen tree and then back to the ground as he turned around to stare at Kaine. "Soon, it will be our turn to have our Rites. I will be an Arcblader, I know it." Solen grinned at Kaine, as if waiting for Kaine to respond.

For a heartbeat, Kaine struggled to remember the response, his throat tight with old emotion. Then, as he had every time they spoke of the Rites in their youth, he answered, "I will be the mighty Hunter of Ara, I will lead all other Hunters."

Solen had wanted the role that Kaine had been chosen for, an Arcblader, protector of Ara. Solen turned to look at him as they strolled. "I'll protect our home while you venture out to do Ara's bidding. You'll always have a place to stay with Lizbet and myself."

"Lizbet?" Kaine jerked his head, frowning at his friend.

"Of course, she is my intended." Solen was so busy staring ahead at the sparkling lights that were flickering through the leaves, he didn't notice the frown on Kaine's face. "It's starting, let's go." Solen swatted at Kaine and then ran to go watch the ceremony of the Rites at Sala Way. Kaine followed, unsure what was happening but liking the fact that he was with his best friend again. Did Gaia send him back in time?

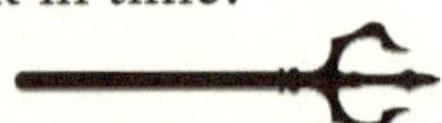

"Can anyone see anything?" Eon asked as he moved along the cool, damp, stone wall. "Guys- oomph!" Eon rubbed his forehead where he could feel a bump forming, glaring at the wooden door that appeared in front of him from nowhere. "What the-?" The question lodged in his throat as the door opened.

"Hey little dude, you shouldn't use your head to knock."

Eon stared up at Draken who was smiling down at him, while he stood there with his mouth agape.

"Come on in, kid." Draken chuckled and ruffled his hair as he pulled him inside. "Kimi made some cookies, I'm betting if you check, there is some chocolate chip just for you." Before Eon could say anything, he heard Calton crying out. "Be right back, daddy time." Eon watched as Draken shifted into his blue dragon, flying over the couches and down the hallway.

"Draken!" Eon heard Kimi holler from the kitchen. "Don't shift in the house, you'll break something!" Right after she shouted that, there was a crash down the hallway, followed by a muted apology from Draken and a groan from the kitchen.

Eon realized that he was standing in Draken and Kimi's home. All around him he saw familiar sights, sights he remembered from his visits from so long ago. The large sea shell from the first time that Kimi and Draken had met. Draken created a lamp out of it for Kimi. The picture of Draken and Rikar in the wooden frame stood on the desk, just as it had long ago. He started to move to the kitchen, where he could smell the chocolate chip cookies, his favorite.

He stopped when he saw his reflection in Kimi's mirror, the only gift she had ever received from her mother, Aphrodite. He was once again the child god who refused to grow up.

"Eon!"

He turned to see Kimi walk into the room, a plateful of cookies in her hands. "Kimi." He nodded in greeting, though he was unsure of what was happening.

"Really?" She set the cookie tray on the table nearest to the couches with a smile. "Since when have you ever been so proper?"

"Uh-"

She laughed at the confusion on his face before she turned to smile lovingly at Draken who appeared with the infant Calton in his arms. "Draken could take some pointers from you." She winked at the silent Eon, who watched them embrace. How could he be here?

Rikar moved through the darkness with ease, not pausing in his movements, even as the world darkened around him. He stepped out into the light and water rushed around him until he was completely submerged. In front of him stood his father's castle.

"Let's get this over with." He turned to see his brother floating next to him in the water with a grim expression. "This will be the last time that the old man summons us like this."

Rikar watched his brother swim to the castle, his words ringing in his head like an omen. He remembered this day; the day Poseidon summoned them. The day his brother and Poseidon had that fateful argument. They were never summoned again.

He swam quickly to the castle, entering while his

father's guards stood there with their lances, not even acknowledging his presence. He raced through the halls; the water kept at bay by his father's magic. Upon entering the throne room, there stood his brother and father, glaring at each other.

"You will do as I say!" Poseidon's voice thundered around the castle in his anger.

"No, father. I will not let you manipulate my life. You don't get to choose who I mate with." Draken stood up to their father, his body glistening with his power and anger.

"The seers have informed me that if you and Calista bear a child, that child will have unimaginable powers." Poseidon grew in size as he spoke, his eyes boring into Draken, but Draken didn't back down.

"I don't know why you would care about a child of mine; you won't have anything to do with any of my children," Draken told him before turning and stalking away.

"Don't you turn your back on me!" Poseidon roared but Draken never paused as he moved past Rikar who stood there silently. Poseidon turned to Rikar and demanded. "Talk some sense into that brother of yours!"

Rikar glared at him. "You're no father, you only care about yourself. They could've been happy if you would've kept your ego out of their lives." With those words he turned to follow his brother from Poseidon's castle.

A light shined from the darkness that Calista walked through. No one spoke from the time they entered the darkness; she didn't know if they were still there or if Gaia had separated them. She moved forward, refusing to back down, or pause to find the others. She stepped out of the darkness, her breath catching as sunlight spilled across her face for the first time in what felt like ages. Before her stretched a shoreline bathed in gold, waves whispering against white sands.

Along the beach, mortals ran and splashed in the surf, dressed in the loose tunics and sashes of a world long gone. A world where mortals believed and worshipped the gods of old. She walked along the coast, the hum of divine energy thrumming beneath her skin. Mortals bustled in the distance, their laughter echoing through the stone streets. She looked past their homes and saw the marble towers of the gods that gleamed, radiant and alive with magic.

This was Atlantis.

Not the drowned kingdom she came to know but the living city before the curse; the one that woke each morning to the kiss of the sun. With barely a thought, she shimmered from the beach to appear right in front of Rowena's gleaming white marble temple. She laughed as she looked around and saw her family; the gods of Atlantis.

Rowena stood in the open doorway of her temple, a happy contented smile as she observed all around her.

Malis guided warriors in training, her silver headpiece flashing with every turn. Beside her, Cael's laughter rang out as he conjured illusions of shimmering birds that danced through the air. Her parents looked so happy, as if they never felt the bitter taste of betrayal. Atmos stood nearby, sketching the moment into existence, while Malov watched everyone, her eyes soft with eternal wisdom.

Salis greeted passing farmers with a blessing, his armor etched with symbols of wheat and harvest. Lison wove garlands of sea-flowers while chipmunks nestled in her red hair. Brine and Stratos debated the merits of peace, one teasing and light, the other solemn as ever. Tylaos watched it all with the quiet patience of time itself, his smile faint but kind.

Even Brax was there, watching everyone silently from the shadows, his eyes hooded and face unreadable.

It was perfect. Too perfect.

CHAPTER 8

Livinia strolled through the darkness, her body belying the tenseness beneath, brewing in wait while she scanned her surroundings. Not with her sight, but all her other senses that were heightened in this darkness that surrounded her. Her braids lay passive against her, as if they were nothing more than hair, but each strand combined with another in readiness to strike if needed.

A light shone broke through the darkness before her, she paused, her braids moving slightly, but she sensed no threats. Her body straightened and she moved with purpose to the light, though her entire being still prepared for a fight if needed.

"Relax dark one."

Livinia turned slowly to stare into the darkness from behind her. "You call me the dark one, yet you're the one who is hiding in the shadows."

From the shadows a figure emerged into the light, yet it seemed the light didn't touch her. The ground beneath her darkened with each step. Her dark hair flowed around her while her pale skin glowed with ethereal beauty. Livinia's eyes narrowed on the crescent moon staff the woman carried.

"You're the one who sent Calista on this mission of hers," Livinia stated, to which the dark head of the goddess nodded. "Why are you here?"

"You're an enigma to all here. You're not a daughter of Gaia, nor any of her ethereal siblings," Nyx spoke softly, her gaze not leaving Livinia. Livinia wasn't sure if it was an intimidation tactic, or something else, though she refused to show any weakness. That wasn't her way, so she stayed silent, her gaze steady under Nyx's stare.

A few more moments of silence before Nyx gave a nod of her head and moved forward, slowly walking past Livinia as she spoke. "What is the name of your Empyrean?" Nyx asked her.

Livinia watched Nyx, who was still walking away without looking back as she spoke. "I'm part of the assassin class of my world, not the spiritual. I don't even know if they are able to speak to our world as those of your world does."

"The number of those who still communicate with Gaia has dwindled considerably, since the dawn of creation," Nyx admitted. "Mortals have forgotten the reverence that once bound them to their creators. Most live now as though the life they were given, was always their own to claim."

"So, there are still mortals that worship the gods?" Livinia queried as she followed Nyx along the stone path that wove between watery ponds. Ahead of them was a stone temple, though it seemed the light never touched the temple.

"There will always be mortals that worship the gods," Nyx informed her and then admitted. "Though the numbers decrease with time."

Livinia nodded, her braids swaying with her moments.

"It's odd," Nyx said softly, again Livinia stayed quiet as they neared the temple. "I have to admit, you're the first one who's come through that trial without a single regret."

"What trial?" Livinia asked, her face still with no emotion showing, though curiosity flickered behind her calm tone.

Nyx stopped at the doorway to the stone temple and turned to Livinia who paused in her stride. Nyx gave a slight nod to the cave they departed from. "The trial of regret, one your friends still endure."

"Why am I not with them, helping them?" Livinia asked.

"The Trial of Regret is faced alone. No one can intervene." Nyx's gaze dropped to the carved handle before them; a dragon's arched body frozen mid-roar in stone. A shadow fell across Livinia when Nyx turned to look at her. "You have your own trial to face."

"I thought I already passed your little trial." Her braids whispered against her skin, as if restless.

"You passed nothing, there was nothing to pass. You've just moved on to the next trial," Nyx informed her with a neutral expression, though Livinia's expression hardened slightly.

"What trial is that?" she asked.

Nyx motioned towards the door. "Step through, and you'll find out. Unless you'd rather turn back. If so, I'll send you to wait for your friends, but you'll forfeit any chance of an audience with Gaia, even if they succeed."

With a tightening of her lips, Livinia reached for the handle, twisting the dragon and entering the stone temple.

Nyx watched the heavy doors seal with a hollow thud. "You may walk without regret," She murmured, her voice echoing in the darkness that flowed out around her, swallowing her. "But tell me, can you walk without fear?"

Kaine stepped out of the forest to see all of the nations of Ara gathered in Sala Way, the only place on Ara where all four nations can gather comfortably. Lava and water will dance with one another and lay under the shade of a tree atop an icy cliff. The air full of magic and nostalgia as Kaine closed his eyes and breathed in deeply, wishing this was more real than a memory. He missed his home, the magic that he had taken for granted until it was stolen from them all.

"Kaine!" Solen hissed at him.

Kaine jerked to see an older Solen standing on one of the raised boulders around the pool at Sala Way. The last time he had been here, had been after that fateful battle, when he had to say goodbye to his friend. There was no sign of that battle now, it looked just as it had that day that both Kaine and Solen had their Rites.

"Kaine!" Solen hissed again. This time he looked around to see his family and others frowning at him as well. They weren't here to watch a Rite; they were here for their Rites. Within the few minutes it had taken Kaine to reach Sala Way, the years had passed so that it was now time for their Rites. The Rites that would see Solen taking the mantle of Hunter and him Arcblader.

He shook his head; he didn't want to step up on the boulder. Solen becoming Hunter had been why the Ancients wanted him, he would lose his friend all over again.

"Move!" He turned around to see his sister, Brooke, pushing him towards the boulder next to Solen. He stumbled and slowly took his place. He looked around to see the other factions taking their places as well, to participate in their Rites. He looked over at Solen but Solen was busy looking into the pool in front of them where water, ice, fire and leaves swirled together as one. He knew what was going to happen when the elements rose and surrounded them. He didn't have to wonder.

The Picknies took their places behind their people, he turned to see Sanders give him a nod and smile. He wondered if the leader of the Aggies knew that he was an illusion, that he lost his life in the final battle of Ara.

He watched the replay as fire surrounded those from the Pyre nation, the Karkens cheering as their symbols appeared to announce their gifts from Ara. Water floated around the Puras while the Carpes blew bubbles in celebration. Ice flakes floated around those from the Floe nation as the Jinsons threw more flakes into the air. It was only him and Solen from Terrane nation, he watched the leaves move from the pool and float around them both. Solen looked above them, his eyes showing the disappointment of not seeing the Arcblader symbol above his head, instead the two bows shined brightly.

Kaine closed his eyes as the cheers from the Aggies and all of Ara rang out around them. His chest tightened with emotions that threatened to choke him. The sound of the celebrations around them started to dim until all was silence, only then did Kaine open his eyes. Gone was Sala Way, though he never once moved. Gone were the nations of Ara as well as all her Picknies. Only Solen stood there, facing away from Kaine.

Kaine looked around and saw that he was still on Ara, though this was the Ara that he remembered from the final battle. No life, only barren land.

"There was nothing you could've done to prevent any of it from happening, I wish you could realize that." Solen spoke though he never turned around.

"If our positions had changed, if I had been the

Hunter instead of the Arcblader," Kaine protested. "I could never truly control the power of the Arcblader, if I could've then maybe Draken would still be alive. You would've been a better Arcblader, you could've defeated the Ancients."

A low laugh escaped Solen before he finally turned, eyes glinting like shards of old starlight. "Are you saying that Ara chose wrong?"

Kaine's voice faltered. "With me? Maybe she did. I don't think I deserved her gifts," Kaine looked down as his throat tightened. He only looked up when he felt the weight of Solen's hand on his shoulder. "I should've been the one to die, not you."

Solen's gaze softened. "Everyone stumbles, Kaine. You've seen my failures too."

"But yours didn't cost lives," Kaine protested.

"Not the ones you saw," Solen replied quietly. "We all carry scars we don't show. The difference is what we do after the fall; that's what defines us. Every choice I made, right or wrong, shaped me into who I was. Your friend. Your brother in arms."

Kaine gave a shaky nod but stayed silent as he listened to his best friend.

"You didn't kill Draken," Solen continued. "He made his choice when he stepped into that beam. He chose to save your life. If you let guilt devour you, then his sacrifice dies with you too." He drew in a slow breath, voice deepening. "As for my death, you had no more power to stop it than Calista did. I would give my life for either of you. That was my purpose and I fulfilled it. I became the man I was meant to be. One my family could be proud of."

The air grew colder, shadows curling at the edge of the world. Solen began to fade, his voice echoing like a fading star.

"You were always meant to bear the Arcblader's light," he said, his form dissolving into the dark. "Stop cursing the gift that chose you. Believe in yourself, Kaine, just as I always have."

Eon sat curled up on one of the overstuffed chairs, eating a chocolate chip cookie while listening to Draken and Kimi telling him about Calton's latest show of power. Seems he saw Draken shifting and tried it. Though he could only shift a tail, Draken said it showed he had great power considering his age. Kimi replied it showed that he needed to have more control since he did it while she was changing him.

Eon laughed so hard he toppled from the chair, clutching his stomach as crumbs scattered across the floor. It felt good to laugh like that again, to feel young and free. But when he pushed himself upright, the laughter died in his throat.

The room was empty.

No Draken. No Kimi. No Calton.

The air had gone cold, and silence hung around him.

The house looked wrong. Cobwebs webbed the corners, dust lay thick across the shelves, and the floorboards had lost their polish. Even the air tasted old, heavy with years.

He turned toward the mirror that still hung on the wall. Once brilliant, it was now a ghost of itself; its surface clouded, eaten away by time. The faint pulse of magic that had once gleamed from it was gone, smothered. His reflection stared back; not the laughing boy, but the weary god who had first stepped into the cave. The youth was gone.

"Hello, grandson."

He turned to see his grandfather standing in the open doorway, smiling kindly down at him. Eon looked around him. "What has happened here, grandfather?"

Tylaos moved across the room to sit down on the couch, dust floating around him as he sat. "Kimi left this place long ago, she and Calton moved in with one of her sisters. She couldn't bear the emptiness without Draken, so she prayed every night he would find his way home."

"And then we return to tell her that he's dead." Eon sighed.

Tylaos nodded.

"So, why are you here, grandfather?" Eon asked him.

"The question isn't why am I here, but why are you?" Tylaos asked.

Eon frowned at him. "What do you mean? I'm trying to help Calista get an audience with Gaia."

"But why are you here, in this home that you haven't visited since you left Earth?"

Eon looked around, biting on his lower lip. "It was a happier time." He shrugged.

Tylaos looked around. "Doesn't look too happy right now."

"No." Eon looked down at the dusty wooden floor.

"Come sit with me, Eon," his grandfather invited.

Eon moved slowly to sit with his grandfather. "I miss him, grandfather," he admitted with a heavy tone.

"I know." Tylaos put his arm around him, giving him a gentle squeeze.

"Why couldn't I save him?" Eon felt his eyes burn with tears.

"Because I wasn't meant to be saved."

Eon turned and saw Draken standing there gazing fondly at him. "Draken? You're alive?" His smile fell when Draken gave a sad shake of his head.

"Not in the way you want me to be."

"Is this my penance for not being able to save you?"

"You know, I remember a little impatient god who wanted to master all his abilities at once," Draken reminisced with a grin. "Until his grandfather sat him down and had a nice long chat with him. Do you remember that chat, Eon?"

Eon's lips trembled into a faint smile. "I remember. Grandfather sat me down and told me not to rush my powers. That they'd come when I was ready." He looked up at Draken, frustration flickering again. "I've tried, but why could I save Rikar and not you? I'm the god of time, of new beginnings. I'm supposed to carry my grandfather's mantle one day. So why can't I do something as simple as turning back the clock?"

"Simple?" Tylaos' voice held a low, almost mournful note. "Reversing time is no simple trick. It's the heaviest burden of all my powers." He glanced at Draken, eyes dim with understanding. "To move time backward is to fight the current of creation itself. One thought astray, one flicker of doubt, and the world forgets how to exist."

Draken placed a hand on Eon's shoulder. "You did everything you could, little one. That's all any of us can do, and it was enough. I'm proud of you."

Eon blinked hard, his throat aching.

Tylaos' voice softened. "You'll learn what you're meant to learn, when you're meant to learn it. Until then, be patient with your power. To learn too quickly," he said, "is to outpace your own purpose."

Eon nodded slowly, eyes fixed on Draken. "I understand," he whispered. "But I still miss you."

Draken's smile warmed, the edges of his form already dissolving into light. "Then remember me well, and keep moving forward. Look out for Calton for me, let him know that his father loves him."

The world around Eon began to fade, colors bleeding into shadow until he was alone again; sitting on a swing in a quiet, sunlit park. The wind carried the faint echo of Draken's laughter, and for the first time, Eon let the sound bring peace instead of pain.

CHAPTER 9

Rikar shifted to his dragon and sliced through the water, his destination the caves in Atlantis. He knew that was where his brother would be, they both enjoyed those caves when their emotions were running high. Those caves had given them both purpose during their imprisonment beneath the waves with the other Atlanteans. They had taught Calista in those caves after the curse had lifted and even after Solen had left.

The veil shimmered before him as he neared Atlantis, with a mighty kick of his tail, he sliced through the veil and landed with human feet on the ground outside the caves. He breathed in deeply and entered the caves.

"I'm done with him, Rikar," Draken growled, his hands fisted at his side. "You won't believe what he wanted."

"He wants you and Calista to have a child," Rikar said simply.

Draken turned with a growl. "He ordered me to mate with her and bear a child."

"You love her." Another simple statement from Rikar. "Why let dad ruin it for you? If you love her, then ignore him and get with her."

Draken frowned at him. "Since when have you championed for me and Calista? Weren't you the one who told me to let her go and move on with my life?"

"I was wrong," Rikar admitted. "You love her."

"She doesn't love me," Draken sighed. "She still mopes after that damn Solen."

"She doesn't know how you truly feel for her, tell her," Rikar pleaded. "Tell her how you feel, forget father and his demands. Live your life with Calista, you can help her forget Solen."

Draken shook his head. "It's no use Rikar, even if I were to pursue her, I couldn't be sure if her feelings were her own, or products of his manipulation." Draken scoffed.

"Do you really think Calista could be swayed by anyone?" Rikar persisted.

"NO!" Draken roared and stormed from the cave.

"Draken! Wait!" Rikar called out to him, closing his eyes and falling to his knees. "You can make her forget him!" He whispered. "If you could do that then there would be no need for her to leave or us to follow." He felt the wetness of a single tear that slipped down his cheek as he thought about his brother and his fate in the stars.

"It wouldn't have worked, Rikar."

Rikar leapt up in surprise and turned around to see his brother standing there, though not the same one who had stormed from the cave. This one was the one who followed Calista to the stars. "Draken?"

His brother nodded. "Hello, brother."

Rikar looked toward the cave exit where the brother he'd been pleading with had just left, then back to the one now smiling at him. "Is this truly you?"

Draken nodded.

"I'm sorry, I should've tried to convince you to get with Calista. Then we wouldn't have had to go to space."

Draken chuckled. "You know better than that, brother. You couldn't have changed my mind, no one could. Besides, we both know that Calista and I never belonged together. I've never been happier than I was with Kimie and Calton. Everything worked out, the way it was meant to, even my death."

Rikar closed his eyes and nodded, his chest tight. When he opened his eyes, it was nighttime and he was no longer in the caves. He stood before a lighthouse that shone its light into the darkness.

Calista stepped forward, taking in Atlantis as her family moved among their acolytes and one another. Her father draped her mother in bursts of colorful flowers, earning an eye roll and a quick kiss before she scolded him for interrupting her work with her warriors.

"Mother!" Calista called. "What's going on?"

She reached her just as her mother turned…and walked straight through her.

Calista froze, wide-eyed, her breath catching as others moved through her as if she were air. "What's going on?" she repeated, more softly this time, as her mind tried to make sense of the scene.

"You regret being born. You regret being the cause of the curse that sentenced your family to their watery prison," came a familiar voice.

Calista turned to find Nyx watching her, shadowed and serene.

Licking her lips, Calista looked around again; seeing her family laughing, her mother radiant and alive, her father unburdened. "So, they were never cursed?"

Nyx shook her head.

Calista frowned. "Shaylane's mother, where is she?"

Again, Nyx shook her head.

"But if I was never born, they should all be safe."

Nyx's gaze didn't waver. "You weren't the reason for the Ancients' first descent into Atlantis. That was Trelaine's doing. Your birth had nothing to do with it. Without you, there was no second coming."

"At least they're happy." Calista's voice trembled as she looked upon them. "They get to see the sun."

Nyx said nothing.

Then the sky began to darken. Clouds swelled, thunder rolled, and the sea trembled as light spears struck down from Olympus. Calista screamed as the Greek gods descended upon Atlantis. She ran toward her family, trying to stop the battle, but her hands passed through them like mist. Ares' blade cut through the sky, and Hera's laughter echoed like breaking glass.

"Why?" she cried, turning to Nyx, tears streaking her face. "If I wasn't born, then why did this happen?"

"Ares was angered when your mother rejected him," Nyx said, her tone even, her eyes ancient. "Without you, there were no Ancients to temper his wrath. No one stood against his pride. So, he turned that fury upon Atlantis itself. He and Hera whispered fear into the hearts of the Olympians until even Zeus believed the Atlantean gods a threat. And so, without you… Atlantis burned."

Calista stared at the ruin around her; their bright city collapsing, divine blood staining the sea. Her knees gave way. "I don't understand. I thought I was the problem."

Nyx stepped closer, her voice low and resonant, carrying the weight of eternity. "You were never the problem, Calista. You were the balance. Life will always find reason to suffer, with or without you; but meaning, meaning only exists because you choose to face it."

Calista looked up, trembling.

"You cannot undo what was," Nyx continued, "but you can choose what will be. Regret is a chain that binds you to ghosts, but purpose; purpose sets you free. You were not born to be blameless. You were born to be needed."

The storm quieted. The ruins flickered away like ash in a wind.

Calista rose slowly, her expression soft but sure. "Then I live and I fight."

Nyx nodded in approval as she faded into the darkness. "And fight, you will."

Where Nyx once stood, now stood a feminine creature who towered over Calista, a crown of thorns on her head. Her hair looked like tangled grass and moss, while her body resembled dried mud with cracks spreading all over.

"You can't defeat me, little girl." The dry words were spoken between the dirty lips.

Calista stood, her chin held high and her hands glowing with her power. "I can and I will." She ran towards the queen, leaping in the air, her hands outstretched as she released the energy that built within her at the queen. A screech filled the air as the queen blocked the energy and then swatted at Calista with her arms that were as big as tree trunks with dead branches for fingers. Calista fell to the ground, the breath knocked from her lungs.

"Not so sure of yourself anymore." The mocking laughter of the queen echoed around Calista who groaned as she pushed herself up.

"I'm still here," she spat as she manipulated the air around the queen to harden, putting the queen in a prison that she couldn't see. Calista frowned as the queen sunk into the ground and rose behind her. When Calista turned around to deflect any blow, the queen was several feet away from her, and now she was the one in the invisible prison. "Wha-?" Calista looked around her with a frown while the queen laughed.

Calista dispersed the invisible walls with a wave of her hands, glaring at the queen. "Cute, but I still control what I create."

The queen laughed some more, "we shall see about that."

Livinia moved effortlessly through the darkness of the temple, her braids gliding ahead of her like searching serpents. They brushed against stone, warned her of stairs and archways, and kept her movement fluid. Assassins of her world could not see in pitch blackness as if it were day, but they were never blind. Livinia saw more than most; her braids made sure of it.

She descended the narrow corridor, ascended a short flight of steps, and entered an open chamber. Five steps in, fire ignited along the walls in a ring of sharp light.

Livinia stopped dead. She knew this room. The Red Ledger Room, or a perfect illusion of it.

She scanned it with a slow, cold frown. The raised dais at the front. The high-backed execution-chairs. And the book lying open at the center; the Final Ledger, the record reserved only for assassins who had failed beyond forgiveness.

Her chest tightened. She had not seen this room in years. It was a place for judgment… and erasure.

"Daughter."

Livinia turned slowly.

Her mother entered, tall and regal, emotions muted

behind a mask of training and tradition. She moved with the precision of a blade.

"You're not the leader of the assassins," Livinia said, her tone flat.

Her mother tilted her head. "No?"

"She would never acknowledge our blood tie."

"Unless," her mother said quietly, "she knew it would be the last time she ever spoke to you."

Livinia's brow furrowed, but she stayed silent.

"You've failed us, Livinia." Her mother's voice rang through the chamber as the rest of the council filed inside and took their seats on the Crimson Dais. "You chose outsiders over your own people."

"I completed my mission," Livinia replied, chin held high.

"And then you returned to escort the marked targets to safety," a bald male councilor said, his black eyes fixed on her. "That breaks the spirit of the contract."

"Once a contract is completed, I am free to act as I choose. Those are the Guild's own bylaws." Her voice stayed level. Showing emotion here would be tantamount to confession. And she felt no guilt. Not for them. Not for this.

A female councilor leaned forward, her short-cropped hair casting sharp shadows over her severe face. "In all our recorded history, no assassin has ever wielded the letter of the rules against their spirit. You twist our laws to justify sentiment."

"Just because it hasn't been done," Livinia said, "doesn't make it wrong."

The council murmured in agitation.

"Enough." Her mother's voice cracked like a whip. "We cannot permit one assassin, my daughter or otherwise, to fracture the codes that hold our order together. If you break one law and face no consequence, others will follow. Our system collapses. Our authority shatters. Centuries of order die in a single act of indulgence."

Livinia swallowed. The words were harsh but true, at least to them.

"What is your ruling?" asked the smallest councilor at the far end, her dark curls trembling ever so slightly.

Her mother's expression became stone. "My daughter will serve as the example our people require. She will be confined in the Chamber of Silence for no less than twenty years, after which she may request a hearing for leniency."

The council nodded, their voices echoing around the room in assent.

"We must guard our laws."

"No dissent can be tolerated."

"Defiance is a disease; unchecked, it spreads."

Livinia's stomach turned to ice.

The Chamber of Silence.

A place where magic stripped speech from every tongue. Where dozens might stand beside you and yet you would hear nothing; ever. A prison of living emptiness. Even the strongest assassins had shattered there.

"No."

The word escaped her before she realized she'd spoken it. The entire council stared in open shock.

"What did you say?" her mother demanded. Her composure cracked, irritation breaking through. No assassin had ever dared speak against a ruling in the Red Ledger Room. Families would rather suffer the penalty than stain their reputation with defiance.

Livinia straightened, pulse pounding with fear, and something sharper. Rikar's face flickered across her mind, and her chest tightened with realization.

Her greatest fear was losing him.

This illusion, this trial, knew exactly where to strike.

"I said no," Livinia repeated, voice steady. "I will not accept your judgment. My friends need me. Rikar needs me. And this trial..." she swept a hand toward them. "Is nothing but noise meant to pull me away from what matters."

"You will stand down, daughter!" her mother shouted, fury twisting her features.

"No." Livinia stepped close to her, staring her down despite the inch of height difference. "I give my loyalty freely now. And I do not give it to fear."

Her braids lifted, ready.

Then Livinia moved; vaulting clean over her mother before the council could react.

Guards lunged at her, but her braids snapped like living whips, striking them aside. She tore open the chamber doors and blinding sunlight poured through, warm and brilliant against her skin. She ran toward it, away from judgement, away from fear, and toward the one person she refused to lose.

CHAPTER 10

Rikar moved through the dark stairwell, climbing toward the distant glow above. He didn't know what he was going to find up there, but he knew that was his destination. His resolve hardened with each step up the darkened corridor. A corridor that seemed to get lighter the closer to the top he came.

He stepped out from the corridor onto the top of the lighthouse, but no light shone, no railing around the edges, nothing. He was no longer standing on the lighthouse, he now stood on a cliff, the cliff that overlooked the atoll where Atlantis once basked in the sun. He turned to see his brother standing there with his back towards him. How many times had he come here to see his brother standing in that exact spot?

"Draken?"

His brother turns around and smiles at him. "Hello, brother."

"This is another of Gaia's illusions." Rikar shook his head.

"Probably," his brother admitted, his eyes on Rikar.

"So, what test is this?" Rikar asked dejectedly.

"I was going to ask you the same thing."

Rikar frowned at him. "You're a creation of hers, you should know."

"Actually, I'm a vision from your memory, I know what you know," Draken shot back. "These trials are to prove your worthiness to Gaia before you attain an audience."

"How is seeing my dead brother proving my worthiness?" Rikar asked him. "I see you enough in my sleep, brother."

"I know," Draken spoke with a heavy voice.

"I keep reliving that day, keep seeing that idiot charge the cannon, I wanted to kill him," Rikar spoke looking at the illusion of the Atoll. His chest felt tight and heavy, his throat tightened.

"Was Kaine the one you were truly angry at?" Draken asked.

Rikar gave a shake of his head, finally admitting his deep dark secret. "No, I'm angry at myself. It was my power that the Ancients used in that damn cannon. If I hadn't let them drain me, if I hadn't been so weak, I could've saved you."

"You know better than to think you could stop me from doing anything, little brother." Draken sighed. "There was nothing you could do, I chose my path, now it's time for you to choose yours."

Rikar looked at him. "What do you mean?"

"Are you going to wallow in self-pity or are you

going to join Calista and fight the queen?" His brother stared right at him. Rikar's eyes narrowed on him. "Don't get mad at me, brother. Everything I'm saying, you already know."

Rikar sighed and nodded. "I know, I still miss you."

"I miss you too, one day we will be reunited but not until it's your time," Draken said and then pointed to the right. "Now, you have a battle to join."

Rikar turned to see Calista battling a creature that could only be the Ancient's queen. He frowned and looked at Draken. "Is that truly the queen or another illusion?" he asked.

"Does it matter?" His brother shot back.

Rikar shook his head and shifted into the blue dragon before he took off into the air, flying towards Calista.

The darkness around Kaine started to dissipate and he saw that he was still on Ara. Still the same Ara he left that fateful day with Calista and the others. There stood the crater where Calista lit the fires of Ara one last time, she gave a gift to those who perished in the battle that couldn't be repaid. He moved slowly towards the crater, his feet dragging on the dry ground as he moved, until he stood in front of the crater.

"Hello, Arcblader."

He looked down to see Sanders next to him, looking into the same crater. The leader of the Aggies who perished in that fateful battle, looking just as Kaine remembered him. "Sanders, what are you doing here?"

"I felt you needed me, was I wrong?" Sanders looked up at him from beneath those rainbow-colored bushy eyebrows.

Kaine breathed in deeply. "Will Ara ever heal, Sanders?"

"No one knows, Arcblader," Sanders told him. "Even those who stayed behind to help her heal don't know."

"Can Lizbet truly heal Ara?" Kaine attempted to keep his doubt out of his voice, though even he could hear it.

Sanders sighed, "Everyone knows that she has none of her mother's talents, something that she has always hated and tried hiding."

"That's not giving me much confidence, Sanders," Kaine grumbled.

Sanders gave a shrug. "Would you rather me lie to you?"

Kaine breathed in. "No. I just worry that I'll never be able to return home."

"Even if Ara was able to come back to life, would you still leave your new friends and return home?"

Kaine shrugged. "I don't know, but I would like to find out."

Sanders nodded. "I understand, but are you going to let it interfere with your goal of freeing all from the threat of the queen and her Ancients?"

"No." Kaine shook his head.

"Good, because I believe Calista needs your help."

Kaine looked over to the direction that Sanders nodded to see Calista battling a creature that seemed to dispel into the Earth and then appear behind her. "Is that the queen?" He looked back at Sanders but he no longer stood there. He turned and ran towards Calista, he could see some of the others running as well.

Eon leaned back in the swing and started kicking his legs so that the swing started moving back and forth. Something he hasn't done in a long time now, since he grew in years and left the child behind. He looked around the playground, not seeing anyone he knew.

Not Draken.

Not Rikar.

Not even Calista.

He was alone in this playground, not understanding why he was here. He didn't like these games that Gaia was playing with them, what was the reason? He jumped off the swing and moved to leave the playground but as he reached the edge, he ran into an invisible barrier.

"What is this?" He put up his hand and placed it against the barrier with a frown. His childlike hand. "What is going on?" On the other side of the barrier, he saw a replay of Draken getting hit by that energy blast from the cannon. "NO!" He shouted and started banging on the barrier. "Let me out!" He shouted.

Nothing.

The barrier remained as he watched Draken in Calista's arms, tears flowing down his cheeks as he slammed his fists on the barrier.

He turned around to see the playground, the symbol of the youth he never wanted to let go. He hated growing up because with age comes responsibilities and angst. He thought if he stayed young then he could avoid that. All that happened was that he wasn't around when his family and friends needed him.

He threw back his head and let out a sorrowful wail, a wail so powerful that it shattered the invisible barrier around him. He looked down and saw his fingers that dug into the earth, fingers that were no longer child-like. He stood up and turned to see a dark figure moving towards him.

"Nyx," he acknowledged her.

"Eon." She nodded at him. "Are you ready to throw off the shackles of your youth that you hid behind for so long and join your family?"

He nodded.

"Then go."

He turned towards where she pointed and saw his sister in battle with a creature that looked as if it was created from the terra it stood upon. He conjured a vortex and ran through. He appeared next to Rikar who had just reached his sister.

"Back up!" Calista shouted as she dodged a long

thick vine that slammed into the ground where she had stood only moments before. "I don't want anyone getting hurt." She attempted to manipulate the ground beneath the monster, pulling it down, but only for a moment before the monster rose once again.

"You can't defeat me, little goddess." The monster growled, its wooden tentacles whipping Calista's legs from beneath her.

She hit the ground with a thump and groaned.

"You can't fight this alone," Rikar growled, shifting to dragon and launching at the creature. "You're getting my help whether you want it or not."

Calista rolled over and pushed herself off the ground. She was about to yell at Rikar when she realized the others joined him in the battle. Her chest tightened, she didn't want anyone else to die.

"It isn't your choice, princess." She turned to see Draken standing there. "You can't try to protect everyone."

"Why not?" she asked, swallowing the tears. "I'm tired of people dying because of me."

"Hate to break this to you, princess, but they're not dying because of you. It isn't always about you," Draken told her and she frowned at him. "They're fighting for their own freedom, for the freedom of others. And yes, for their own vengeance. Do you really want to deprive them of that?" She bit her lip and looked down at his words. "Seems kind of selfish to me, maybe living with Ares all those years did have an effect on you."

Calista jerked her head up but Draken was no longer there. She turned to see the others fighting the monster. She gave a nod and joined the frey. Kaine was charging up the ground beneath the monster, who shrieked in pain while Livinia would jump on the head, slashing with her knives while her braids kept the vines from touching her. Rikar inflamed many of the thick vines and her brother would cause many limbs to age and wither.

She ran forward and leapt into the air, her hands glowing with the energy she manipulated. Rikar's tail swung out and wrapped around her chest. He twirled around with her and then released her so that she was moving too fast for the monster to block her. With one big eruption the monster dissolved while they all stood there together.

"Is that it?" Her brother moved closer to her.

"I don't know," Calista admitted and looked around as the scenery changed from a barren wasteland to green flora with waterfalls and ponds.

"You don't know?" Alvia appeared, as if from thin air, his body swaying from side to side as he walked towards them. "That could be your theme song," he grumbled. "If you had one." He gave a shake of his head and continued, "you've all been busy thinking you have to do this by yourself, but you forget that your goals are all the same. If you learn to work together, maybe you could earn a better theme song."

"Never mind Sav, she tends to get touchy when

others aggravate her." Nyx moved from the shadows, her face serene with no emotion.

"Sav?" They turned to see the old man straighten into the woman they met at Stahle's.

She gave a shrug of her shoulders. "One of my preferred forms." Her gaze lingered on them momentarily. "Feel honored." She walked away without waiting for a response.

"Where are you going?" Calista asked her.

Sav turned partly to look at Calista. "Do you want to talk to Gaia or not?"

Calista swallowed and followed her.

Chapter 11

"How did those trials make us worthy to see Gaia?" Rikar growled as he followed Sav past the waterfalls and through a cave entrance.

But it wasn't Sav who answered, it was Nyx.

"You can ask Gaia that when you see her."

Calista raised a brow but said nothing, looking out the side of her eye, she saw Rikar's face tighten. They followed Nyx and Sav in silence, weaving through the dense fauna and past the waterfall into a hidden grotto beyond. Stone walls shimmered with streaks of color, ivy and moss clinging to the rock as water spilled freely into a nearby pool.

Nyx and Sav paused at the entrance, motioning for the others to go on ahead. They circled the grotto, taking in the painted walls that were alive with color and ancient depictions of gods and goddesses. Around them were trees that formed chairs, high backs with colorful foliage.

"Hello."

They turned to see a woman standing there, a very beautiful woman. She exemplified perfection, her ivory skin showed no blemishes and her auburn hair cascaded down her back in waves. She wore robes with earth tones and jewels woven in. When you looked into her eyes, you were mesmerized. It was as if you could see years and years of earth or maybe the creation.

"Gaia," Calista said but stayed where she stood. She wasn't sure what she expected, if she had any expectations, but now that she stood before Gaia, her stomach churned a bit. Though she refused to give any indication that she felt any intimidation.

Gaia looked at her, though she didn't smile. "The Atlantean princess with the checkered past." Calista said nothing and Gaia turned to the others. To Eon she said "the little Atlantean prince who finally grew up."

She looked at Kaine. "The alien child of my sister."

To Livinia. "Your Empyrean is not a sibling of mine, though that does not make him any less powerful. He is not too happy with you, though. He likes to think he has better control over his children." Livinia's brow furrowed slightly though she said nothing.

To Rikar. "The mighty dragon brother." She looked him up and down. "I have truly been interested in meeting you," she told him.

"Why?" He frowned at her.

"For so long, you have always been the one keeping the peace." She smiled at him. "Now, I wonder if you even know what that word means anymore." Rikar's frown deepened, his lips curling up in a low snarl. Gaia laughed. "You might intimidate others with that growl, dragon, but not me."

"I'm not attempting to intimidate, if I was, you would know it," Rikar told her, folding his arms across his chest. Calista gave a silent sigh, Gaia was right, Rikar went from being the peacekeeper to being the angry one. "I want to know why you would put us through those stupid little tests back there," he demanded.

"Stupid?" She raised one of her perfect eyebrows.

Rikar nodded.

"You all went through the trials of regret and fear for a very simple reason," she informed him in her haughty manner.

"And that is?" Rikar demanded when she didn't elaborate.

"Because I deemed it so." She stared at him. "You seem to forget that you came to me, not the other way around. You do not get to demand anything from me, but I can demand all I want from you." She moved towards him, her gown moving across the ground as if she were gliding instead of walking towards him. "You have come to me to ask for my guidance in stopping my sister-"

"Not just stopping your sister but destroying her," Rikar interrupted.

Gaia's head rose as she stared at him. "You think you can destroy her?" she asked.

"As soon as we find her, yes," he told her.

"Such arrogance." Gaia watched him, her eyes narrowing.

"You say arrogance, I say confidence," he shot back.

"I would love to see if you are as capable as you claim," she told him.

"Just point us in the right direction."

"As much as I would love to see you have to back up your words, I do not know where my sister is," she told him.

"Bull." He growled.

Livinia placed a hand on his arm but he still stared at Gaia.

Calista had enough of all this posturing, she moved past Rikar to address Gaia. "How do we find her?"

"I want to know how she can be so powerful but doesn't know where her sister is?" Rikar interrupted.

Calista sighed.

Gaia looked at him, "do you know where your brother is?" The temperature in the grotto dropped several degrees. Calista turned to intercept Rikar and Livinia reached to constrain him but neither were fast enough. He had shifted and lunged for Gaia who stayed where she stood. Just as he almost reached her, vines shot out from the ground and wrapped around him so tightly that he couldn't move, held in midair. She walked closer to him, his growls not fazing her. "I commend your courage but not your intelligence," she told him as she stopped directly in front of him. "Although, I wonder if you were attempting to anger me so that I would put you out of your misery," she mused, and then turned away from him to look at the others.

"Saying that about his brother was uncalled for," Livinia told her.

Gaia nodded. "As was his remark about destroying my sister."

"Your sister killed your brother and other sister," Kaine told her.

"My sister is in pain, has been in pain and is not herself," Gaia countered.

"That doesn't excuse what she's doing," Calista told her. "Nor does it excuse what she's attempting to do. You don't think she wouldn't do the same to you?"

"I never said that she was in the right, or that she did not need to be stopped." Gaia looked Calista over. "Though, I do not believe that the arrogant one will be able to do that."

"One of us needs to," Kaine countered. "Before she destroys someone else's world."

Gaia gave an unhappy look and nodded, though Rikar stayed contained within her vines. "Unfortunately, you are correct."

"Will you help us?" Calista asked her.

Gaia nodded. "I will do what I can, you have gone willingly through the tests and have proven that you have what it takes to go on this journey." Gaia, who had been watching Rikar, turned her gaze to Calista.

"But I wonder if you will have the strength to complete it."

"I'm willing to try," Calista told her, then looked over at Rikar. "But I'll need everyone to do it."

Gaia nodded and freed Rikar with a wave of her hand. He righted himself and glared at her, but she paid him no mind. She moved to a pool of dark blue water that sat in the corner of the Grotto. She waved a hand over the surface and the water started to shimmer brightly until you couldn't see the water any longer; only the bright light. She turned back to them. "The only one who could possibly help you locate my sister, would be her mystic."

"She has a mystic?" Kaine frowned at Gaia.

Gaia nodded. "We all have our own versions of mystics that speak for us to all our children. Before her mind turned against her, my sister had one herself. No one knows what happened to him." She glided over towards another pool that shimmered in the back of the grotto, her fingers moving over the surface, familiar to how Rowena did long ago. Gaia's gaze peered down into the water, her voice sounded soft, so soft they had to strain to hear her. "To find my sister, you must find her mystic. Only he will know where my sister is, only he can tell you how to find her."

"Why can't you?" Calista asked her.

"Because she is my sister," Gaia said simply. "We are unable to turn on one another; we are connected in a way that makes it impossible."

"Then explain your brother."

"That act severed her connection to our father and marked the beginning of her descent into madness."

"How do we find this mystic or whatever he is?" Livinia asked.

Gaia nodded towards the glowing pool of water. "You must enter Aetherfall through this portal. While there, you will look for him, and he will tell you what you need to know."

"What is this place?" Calista looked down with an untrusting look.

"This land is where the dead from all my siblings go, the ones who are our true children. There they all join, though none of the creatures that has followed my sister since her insanity, have been allowed entrance," Gaia spoke, something in her tone belied her serene expression. "You are looking for a male child of my sister, who lived long before her fall."

"Do you have anything more than that to go on?" Calista frowned. "A name or even description?"

"Seek the crown of thorns, where the crossed threads refuse to break, there you will find the one that time itself could not take," Gaia spoke softly, as though the words were not her own.

"What does that mean?" Rikar growled.

Gaia looked around as if waking from a dream. "I know not, but you must hurry, the portal will not stay open long."

"Great." Kaine shook his head. "So, how long do we have?" he asked.

"You will know when it is time to leave," Gaia said as she neared the glowing portal. "You must find the mystic, learn what he knows, and then hurry back here before the portal closes."

"Even better," Kaine groaned.

Gaia turned back to them. "Go swiftly, time is ticking away as we speak."

"I'll go with them." Sav moved forward.

Gaia frowned. "Are you sure, my child?"

Sav nodded. "This is more important than their friend being a jerk." Sav looked over towards where Kaine stood next to Rikar. "Besides, I think they're going to need all the help they can get." She twirled the staff in her hand, the bulb swirling and glittering.

Gaia looked at the staff, then back to Sav, and gave a nod. "If that is your choice, remember you do not have much time."

Sav nodded. "I know, get back here before the portal closes or be stuck in Aetherfall forever."

"Wait! What did you say?" Kaine's eyes widened and his back straightened. "About being stuck in this place forever?"

Gaia turned to him with her serene expression. "You must find this man and return here before the portal closes or you will never leave the land."

"Don't worry, hero." Sav gave him a dismissive

glance. "I'll make sure you make it home in time to catch your nightly girls' flick."

Kaine frowned at her. "Girls' flick? What's that?"

Instead of answering, Sav chuckled and moved to the portal. "Come on, kiddos. Let's go find this guy so you can get out of Gaia's hair." With those words, Sav ran and vaulted into the portal.

Livinia looked at the others and with a lift of her shoulder, she followed Sav.

Eon, who had stayed silent during this exchange, walked calmly over and with a hop, he jumped into the portal and was gone.

Kaine gave a deep sigh before he ran to the portal and jumped in.

Rikar looked from Gaia to Calista, his face showing his distrust, though Calista could see the resignation as well. He moved with purpose to the portal and dove in.

Calista sighed and looked at Gaia who was watching her closely. "Why?"

"Why what, child?" Gaia asked her.

"Why are you helping us destroy your sister?" Calista asked.

"Who says I am helping you to destroy my sister?" Gaia asked her.

Calista frowned and looked at the portal before looking back at Gaia. "That portal will take us to the person who can help us find her, right?" Calista's stomach clenched at the thought that the others might be in danger.

"Of course." Gaia's brow furrowed at her. "I would not allow my acolyte to enter if it was not."

"But that's helping us in our quest to find your sister and stopping her," Calista said, becoming confused.

"I am helping you locate my sister, but I will not help anyone destroy her," Gaia told her. "That is not allowed. As I said, when my sister went against our brother, she lost her connection to our father. I will not make that same mistake."

"Isn't helping us find her the same thing?"

Gaia smiled at Calista. "All I am doing is sending you to talk to someone who might be able to help you in your quest. I will have nothing to do with hurting my sister."

"What's her name?" Calista asked.

"Excuse me?" Gaia frowned.

"Your sister," Calista told her. "What's her name?"

"She lost her name when she lost her connection to our father," Gaia told her sadly. "She has no more connection to anyone that might be able to calm her. We have always been each other's steadying force, something she was denied when she turned on our brother." Gaia turned away from her to the portal, then looked back at Calista. "I would hurry if I were you; the timer started as soon as my Acolyte entered the portal."

With one last look at Gaia, Calista turned and dove into the portal, not knowing what would be on the other side.

CHAPTER 12

Stepping into the portal, Calista held her breath, as if she were diving beneath the dark water. The surface of the pool swallowed her instantly, light closing around her in a way that felt too deliberate to be natural. At least, that was how she felt; an unknown was an unknown, no matter the circumstances, and those were never truly gentle.

Colors twisted around her; slow spirals of fractured light, too vivid, and too alive. They pressed in from every side, pulling her forward whether she wanted to move or not. Ahead, a brightness waited for her, sharp and unwavering. She moved forward, releasing the breath she had been holding, as a warning echoed unbidden in her mind.

"Stay away from the light!"

Jake's voice shouted in her mind, clear as a memory, half-joking, half-serious. Her old commander said that often, usually with a laugh, and usually right before he threw that ridiculous spongy man from his desk at anyone who irritated him at the time. The thought flickered, almost comforting. Almost.

Then the light engulfed her completely and all thoughts of her past co-workers disappeared. She hit the ground hard, instinct curling her body as she rolled. The surface beneath her wasn't stone, nor was it soil. It felt faintly warm and hummed beneath her skin. She rose from her roll immediately, fluid and ready, dropping into a crouch as her eyes swept the unfamiliar terrain.

The air felt wrong. Too still. Too aware. Of course, she had never been to this land before. The land of the dead that Gaia called Aetherfall. She looked around and saw colorful veins pulsing faintly through the dark earth. Shapes moved at the edges of her vision; floating, drifting, and watching. When nothing approached her, she slowly rose.

She steadied her breath, every sense alert to dangers in this unknown land. This place that no living being was meant to enter. She had a feeling that Aetherfall knew they were here, the bigger question is, what would this land do?

Kaine's laughter had her turning around. "A bit edgy, are we, Calista?"

Calista rolled her eyes, but Eon snorted before she could respond. "This coming from the man who entered with glowing hands, looking ready to attack anyone or anything." Kaine glared at him, but Eon only grinned back.

It seemed the trauma from the trials had abated, though she could see some shadows in the faces of her friends. Especially Rikar, who watched the exchange silently with a dark look. She wondered what trials he had gone through, though her thoughts were interrupted by the sound of a stampede heading their way.

They all looked around but saw nothing, though the sound was getting closer.

"What is that?" Calista looked at Sav, who wore the same confused look as everyone else.

"Why are you asking me?" Sav frowned at her.

"Aren't you our guide?" Kaine frowned back at her.

Sav snorted. "I've never been here before."

"So, why did you come?" Eon asked her.

"I was curious." She shrugged, twirling the staff in her hands as she looked around. "No one is allowed into Aetherfall without a just cause."

"So, you decided to ride our coattails." Rikar's eyes became dragon, his voice harsh as his body shimmered, and scales appeared. "I can't tell you how happy it makes me that we were able to accommodate your curiosity. Now how about you finding us an actual guide," he finished on a threatening growl.

One that Sav ignored.

Calista looked around them, but there was still nothing. The land around them was flat with no fauna or anything, but still, they saw nothing.

Rikar let out a frustrated growl, looking down at his body where only a few scales remained. "What in hades is going on?" He almost shouted, his hands balled into fists, held out from his body. Kaine and Eon frowned at him, while Livinia stared with furrowed brows.

"Having issues there, big boy?" Sav smirked at him.

Rikar's gaze hardened as he stared at her. "Why can't I shift here?" He demanded.

Sav shrugged. "Maybe because this is the land of the dead, think of that?"

Calista shook her head, looked at Sav, and asked, "thought you had never been here before?"

She shrugged. "I haven't, that was just a guess."

Before any of them could say anything, the stampede sound rushed upon them and with the sound was dust that blinded and choked them. When the air cleared and they all were in a fighting stance, they looked around but saw nothing.

"What the-?" Kaine frowned.

"Yip! Yip!"

They looked down to see a fluffy ball running around with a long spiny tail that had two long spikes at the end. Eon leaned down and ran his fingers through the fur and the creature rolled over on its back with its clawed feet flailing in the air. "Where did you come from, little guy?" Eon grinned down at him.

Kaine looked down at the ball of fluff that wiggled around while Eon petted it. "That couldn't have made all that noise. It had to be something else."

"Why do you say that?" Sav asked him.

"He's too little."

"Don't believe your eyes." They jerked around to see a small, wrinkly, old looking man who hobbled up to them, using a gnarled cane. "That little thing is a whole lotta trouble." The man wheezed as he reached them and glared at the puff ball.

Eon looked up at him, still kneeling down and giving the fluff ball attention. "Is he yours?"

"Mine?" The old man frowned. "Naw, Jefro doesn't belong to anyone." The man spoke in a very gravelly voice as he looked over each of them as they gave Jefro uneasy looks. "I wouldn't worry about Jefro, the one you should be worrying about is the Arbiter of Aetherfall."

"Why is that?" Kaine asked him, looking around them.

"The Arbiter doesn't appreciate interlopers," the man told them as he continued to hobble around them, examining them as if he was a drill sergeant looking over new recruits.

"Ummm.. excuse me, mister... What is your name?" Eon asked.

The old man stopped and turned to look at him for a few moments before he answered. "My name is Herman." Then he went back to looking them over.

"Mister Herman," Eon started to say but paused when Herman shook his head.

"Just Herman." The old man stared at Eon, who fidgeted beneath the hard stare. Finally, Eon nodded and Herman went back to analyzing all of them.

"Why does the Arbiter have against visitors that come here?"

Herman's brow furrowed. "Visitors? I said interlopers." Herman harshly tapped his walking stick on the ground twice. They watched as some multi-colored vines rose and crafted a wooden bench for Herman to climb up on before he continued. "This is the land of the dead, when the living enters that puts things off balance. The Arbiter doesn't like things off balance. Only the dead are allowed to enter." He stared at them from his seat.

"So, where is this Arbiter?" Calista asked him. "Is there any way that we can avoid this person?"

"Highly unlikely," Herman drawled with an amused expression. "The Arbiter knows all that goes on in Aetherfall, the minute you touched the ground, he knew."

"So, where is he?" Rikar growled.

Herman turned his hard gaze on Rikar. "Right here."

"You're the Arbiter?" Sav asked him, her body tensing and her grip on her own staff tightened.

"Yes, child of Gaia, I am." Herman looked back at her, placing both his hands on the top of his walking stick. A seemingly innocent gesture, but his words belied that thought.

Rikar moved forward, his eyes narrowed on Herman as his skin rippled once more. "Are you the reason I can't shift?" Livinia moved closer to him, not attempting to stop him, but looking ready to help if needed.

Herman watched Rikar, but showed no reaction

to the formidable visage that Rikar was giving off. "If you're attempting to intimidate me, then you haven't been listening, dragon." Herman's fingers moved slightly. "There is no one in Aetherfall that is more powerful than I. The reason that you can't shift is simple."

Rikar glared when he didn't continue. "And that is?" He growled but attempted to ease back when Herman raised a brow at him.

"This is the land of the dead," Herman told him. "No living beings are allowed here, so no abilities or powers are allowed here."

"So, you're saying that if Gaia or one of her siblings were to come here, that they would be powerless as well?" Calista asked him, then regretted it when he turned his gaze onto her.

"Why would they need to come here?" he asked her. "They have me to take care of Aetherfall, they have no reason to enter here."

"So, you're saying they've never been to Aetherfall?" Eon asked.

Herman shook his head. "Nope, no need. I take care of Aetherfall and ensure that their children that they send here are cared for."

"So, this is where all the dead of the four empyreans go?" Livinia asked.

Herman hopped down from his bench to hobble over to her, ignoring Rikar who moved closer to her. "No, only the ones they choose to send here. And you, dark one, are not a child of any of my empyreans. Why are you here?" he asked her then turned his gaze to Rikar. "Or do I already have my answer?" He mused.

"Don't worry about her." Rikar frowned at him.

"Funny, your brother described you as the fun loving one," Herman said on a sigh. "Seems he didn't know you as well as he thought he did."

"You've spoken to my brother?" Rikar asked him and looked around, his hardened stance softening at the thought of seeing his brother once again. "He's here?"

Herman turned back to him. "I'm the Arbiter of Aetherfall, I speak with all the dead that enter; past, present and sometimes even those who aren't scheduled yet." He looked over them all, then back to Livinia. "Though, I must admit, this is the first time I've spoken with one who isn't on my list. But yet, here she is." Sav moved forward, but paused when Herman turned to her. "Child of Gaia, you have something to say?"

Sav gave a small bow, no smart remark, only one of reverence. "Arbiter, we were sent here by Gaia herself."

"Is that so?" Herman asked her, one eye narrowed on her while the other was opened wide. When Sav nodded, Herman held out his hand. Sav took the bauble off her staff and handed it to him. Herman looked into the bauble with an intent gaze before his eyes widened and he looked at them with a grin. "Looks like you have a mission, a timed one. So, let's get you to your destination so we can get you out of here." With that said, he tossed the bauble back to Sav.

CHAPTER 13

"You go from doom and gloom to happy to help?" Kaine frowned at him.

Rikar watched him through a narrowed gaze, arms crossed, and his body alert.

Herman barely paid Rikar any attention, though he did turn to Kaine and respond. "No, I go from debating on making you permanent residents here, to deciding to help you on your quest. But then again, if you don't need my help…" Herman lifted a shoulder and started to amble away from them.

"Wait!" Calista called out to him, tossing Kaine an aggravated look. "He didn't mean no disrespect." She gave Kaine a very pointed look, one that said to stay quiet. Kaine stared back at her and grinned. She sighed and looked back at Herman, who watched the interaction with something close to amusement.

"I'm sure he didn't," Herman replied sardonically, then shrugged. "But, since I want all of you gone from here, I'll still help." Herman sent a sideways look towards Kaine. "Just make sure to not make me rethink about making you permanent residents." He turned towards Calista. "How can I help?"

"Can you help us find an Ancient who lived long ago before their queen went bonkers." Kaine grimaced.

"An ancient what?" Herman frowned at him.

"An Ancient mystic who served the queen before she started kidnapping people and trying to kill her siblings," Eon told him.

"Queen?" Herman tilted his head.

"Yes, the queen who rules the Ancients. The Ancients are the ones who've been trying to enslave us," Calista informed him.

"Ancients? Don't know no Ancients," the old man mused.

"Then you're no help to us." Rikar growled.

"Really? You don't want help from the Arbiter of Aetherfall?" The old man shrugged and turned away. "In that case, have fun wandering blindly around here, makes no never mind to me if you are stuck here. I'm sure I can find some cage to throw you in."

Calista frowned. "You don't even know who the Ancients are, how can you help us?"

"There is no one here called the Ancients, I would know if there were." Herman turned back and crossed his arms.

"What about the queen?" Eon asked.

"What queen?"

"Never mind," Ryker grumbled and turned to Sav. "Do you have any idea on how we go about finding this male that Gaia is wanting us to find? The mystic of her sister."

"Would that be the mystic of Ara or Leva?" The old man asked them.

They all looked at each other, their brows furrowed. "Who is Leva?" Calista asked him.

"A sister of Gaia," the old man told them.

"The queen?" Rikar asked him.

Herman raised a brow at him. "I told you, I don't know of any queen. I'm the keeper of this realm. I care for the dead of Gaia, Jaru, Ara and Leva." Herman gave a shake of his head. "Such a human term, queen. No Empyrean would lower themselves to use such a term."

"Don't know what to tell you, but that is what the Ancients called her." Eon shrugged.

"Who are these Ancients you keep talking about? I'm the most ancient being you will find in here." Herman watched them.

"You would know them if you saw them." Kaine grimaced. "Silver colored, no expressions, and no emotions at all."

Calista stayed silent, her mind thinking about the times she saw the Ancients show emotions. Usually, frustration and anger when they weren't getting their way, but they would move quickly to disguise such emotions.

Herman gave a shake of his head. "No one here that looks like that."

Rikar snarled and moved towards Herman but Calista intervened and asked him instead. "Can you help us find the Mystic of Leva?"

The old man looked at her. "Why are you wanting to talk to him?"

"We're trying to find Leva and hoping he can help," Livinia answered while Rikar glared at the man.

"Why are you wanting to find her?" The old man looked at them suspiciously.

"Because-" Rikar started but Calista interrupted.

"Ara has sent us to find her."

The old man looked at Calista with a frown. "I thought you were sent by Gaia?"

Calista sighed. "Ara sent us on our original quest to find the queen...Leva..." Calista corrected herself when Herman frowned at her. "We've been... searching for her through the stars with no luck. When we came home to see our family, we were sent Gaia's way to see if she could help, and she sent us here," Calista finished, holding out her hands.

Herman stared at her for a few moments then he lifted his shoulders. "Then, let's go find Minnow."

"Minnow?" Calista frowned at Herman who had already started to amble away, using the cane to keep himself from falling.

"That is the name of the last Mystic of Leva that entered this realm." Herman started to walk with the ball of fluff following, running around his legs without tripping him. He turned when they didn't follow him. "I thought you guys were wanting to talk to the man, you should hurry, time keeps ticking away."

"Do you know if this Minnow has a thorny crown?" Sav asked him.

Herman took a deep breath and sighed heavily. "What is it with you guys and crowns and titles?" He gave a frustrated shake of his head. "There is no need for titles or symbols here, even for the mortals that once held them in life. Here, in the land of the dead, they no longer matter. Once their physical form has passed, they have no need of them. The only one in this land with any power or influence is me, and I need no crown, thorny or golden." He gave them all a hard stare. "Now, if you would follow me to where the children of Leva now reside, you can speak with Minnow. If he isn't the one you seek, maybe he knows how to find this person." When they said nothing, Herman gave a satisfied nod and started ambling towards a moving path that glittered.

"I hope everyone we meet isn't as cranky." Eon spoke low to Calista, who just shook her head.

Unfortunately, Herman heard him, and paused to look back at them over his shoulder. "Thought you guys were in a time crunch?" He grumbled. "Do you want to find this guy before you're returned back to Gaia? Or worse, stuck here forever? If you want to be stuck with me, then keep taking your time. If not, follow me and keep up." That said, Herman continued towards the colorful path.

Kaine looked over at Sav. "Are you two related?"

Sav shrugged, but said nothing as she started after Herman to the moving path. After a brief moment they all looked at one another and started towards the path themselves. When Herman stepped onto the path, it seemed to pause in movement, but still glowed. Each time one of them stepped onto the path, the path would glow brightly before dimming until the next one stepped up. Once they all stood there, the path started to move once again.

They watched the scenery around them change as the path moved them through Aetherfall. The trees bloom with such vibrance that the air crackled. Flowers peeked out from tall blades of grass that rustled as if pushed aside by a furry friend moving about. There were rivers of blue that sliced through the land and weaved into a sea of water where dolphins frolicked. It seemed so peaceful that it brought a smile to Calista's face.

Within moments the landscape changed to the colorful forests of Ara, where Calista was sure that she could see the eyes of the Aggies peering at them from beneath the colorful flora. Past the trees were the unforgiving frigid icy fields where they could see the blue-skinned Jinsons moving with ease, while playing in the cold. Water and fire met past the ice, but not in battle, more like friends who embraced one another in familiarity. The Picknies from both nations ran around, looking at them as they passed by.

"Home," Kaine breathed as he stared out. Calista

felt her body tense, she peered around, on one hand praying to see Solen, but on the other hand scared of that possibility. Could she see the man she loved and still want to leave here to finish what they started? She looked over towards Rikar, who was staring with the same expression. He turned to look at her, she didn't wonder if he was thinking of his brother, the pain she saw there already told her. Her throat constricted and her chest tightened. Life could be so unfair.

Herman nodded but didn't pause. "And Leva is coming up, just past Jaru."

Just as Herman finished his words, Eon gasped and pointed. Calista turned to see a fish flying through the air, its fins twirling over its head. It dove and weaved lazily through the air on invisible currents that none of them could see. She frowned, turned her head only to see birds swimming through rivers, their feathers slicing through the water as though it were their natural element. Upside down trees with roots that reached for the sky, while hairy mammals soared through the air, and foxes with many eyes played with a frog that had eight hairy legs.

"I bet Vesper would love this place." Eon moved to stand next to his sister, wide eyes looking at the chaotic world around them. She said nothing, but nodded in agreement with her brother. Vesper, the Atlantean God of Chaos, would definitely love this place.

"Here comes Leva." Herman nodded forwards. Not

even moments after he said that, the world around them changed. The colorful trees and fauna turned into crystals. The world around them shined and glittered. "Time to get off." Herman stepped off the path and the others jumped when they realized that rather than stopping, the path had kept moving.

"Oomphh!" Kaine grunted when he hit a crystal rock. He sat up and looked around with a frown. "This is the world of Leva?" He frowned. "Is that snow?" He pointed to the whiteness all around them.

"Nope." Herman dusted off his pants. "Leva is a world of crystals, and here is where you will find any of her children, though it has been a very long time since any of them had come here to rest."

"Where would we find the latest ones that arrived?" Sav asked as she rose to her feet, her legs mildly shaky.

Herman shrugged. "Around here somewhere, it isn't like stocking food in a grocery store, all the newest ones in the front and the outdated pushed to the back." Calista looked at Eon, their expressions both confused, but Herman continued before they could comment. "Let's go, time is running out," Herman told them as he moved down the path through the forest.

"We haven't even been here an hour yet," Calista protested as she followed him.

Herman snorted. "You've been here much longer than that. I had to take you through the other levels to get you here, that takes a long time."

"But it didn't feel like it to us." Eon frowned.

"Did you want to actually feel it in real time?" Herman shook his head. "Thought you were here on Gaia's orders, I doubt she wanted you here to get lost in the different lands." He moved through the forest, leaving them to follow quickly so as not to lose him. The trees opened up into a village with crystal houses, fences and even crystal animals running around.

"Is this where the mystic is?" Kaine asked. They all looked around, but the crystal animals were the only movements they could see. They didn't see anyone, not even silver colored Ancients.

"If we find someone wearing a thorny crown, we can bet that would be him." Calista nodded.

"Where are the people here?" Rikar frowned looking around as he walked along paths between the homes.

"Who's asking?"

They turned to see a woman watching them from the doorway of the home that was closest to the forest. She leaned against the door jamb, watching them closely. The only thing silver on her was her hair and eyes, other than that, she could pass as a mortal from Gaia or even Ara. Until you get down to her hands, where her nails looked like diamonds glittering. When she moved though, her skin started to sparkle, then the color blended with several different shades.

"We were sent by Gaia to find the Mystic of Leva," Sav told her.

The woman raised a crystal brow, looked over at Sav, and spoke with a bored drawl, "still doesn't answer my question."

"My name is Calista." Calista moved forward to introduce herself, seeing the widening of Sav's eyes and not wanting things to get tense. She nodded at Sav and then gestured to the others as she introduced them. "That is Sav, then you have Livinia, Rikar, Kaine, and Eon." Each one gave a slight nod when she spoke their name. "What is your name?" she asked.

"Tawnee." The woman nodded. "There are many mystics around here from Leva, from many different times and lineages. Do you know the exact one you're looking for?" she asked them.

"How about the last one to enter here," Rikar suggested. "Unless you know of one who wears a thorny crown."

Tawnee frowned at him, then sighed and pointed down a crystal path. "I don't know anything about a thorny crown, but if you go that way, you'll find a couple of know-it-alls who might." She gave a wry grin.

Calista looked down the path. "Thank you." She turned but Tawnee was already gone. She looked at the others and took a deep breath. "I guess we follow the path."

"You think?" Herman ambled past them and started down the path. "You guys just make friends wherever you go, don't you?"

Calista frowned and looked at the others. "Where did he come from?"

Kaine snorted. "You wanna ask him?" She gave a shake of her head. "Didn't think so. Let's follow the crystal road, shall we?"

Eon grinned and moved forward. "Maybe we'll find a treasure at the end of it, it is as colorful as a rainbow, after all."

"I would settle for a mystic," Rikar said. The others nodded as they moved forward down the road, where Herman was already several feet ahead of them.

CHAPTER 14

"This is beautiful." Kaine looked around at the buildings as they walked. The path from the forest took them into a crystal city with tall shimmering buildings of all shapes and sizes. A whole world made out of crystal, but yet when the sun shone brightly down, they weren't blinded as you would expect.

Calista ran her fingers through the crystal leaves of a bush as they moved past, expecting the rough feel of crystal, but instead felt the softness of leaves. Looking up she saw Rikar staring at her, she held up her hand with one single crystal leaf laying there. He took the leaf and his eyes widened as he realized it wasn't hard.

"Nothing is as it seems," Rikar murmured and she nodded in agreement.

"That's for sure."

"Wow!" Eon's words had them turning to see what had surprised him and saw people walking through the streets of the city, into buildings and sitting on crystal benches. They resembled the woman they met back in the forest. The same silver hair, eyes, and nails but their skin color all were of different hues. Each person would have skin that were different shades of a certain color, they were simply beautiful.

"Nothing like the monotone color and demeanor of the Ancients we first met." Rikar looked over at Calista. She nodded in agreement as she watched them and listened to them speaking to one another. Their voices spoke in volumes and had different tones, though they did sound very musical.

"They don't seem surprised to see us." Livinia looked around, her dark eyes taking in everything around her. She was correct, they didn't act surprised to see them, in fact, they didn't even acknowledge their presence.

"Can they see us?" Kaine asked.

"The one in the beginning did," Eon pointed out.

"True." Kaine nodded.

"While most of the inhabitants here stay in their respective home territories, they are allowed to freely move between the realms," Herman told them as he kept moving forward. "They are used to seeing others from other realms in their city. He gave a sideline look over at Livinia. "Even if one of you isn't from any of these realms, they accept any visitors."

"Definitely different from descendants then," Calista muttered. "The Ancients aren't accepting of anything that doesn't fit with their narrative."

Herman shrugged. "I don't know anything of these Ancients you speak of, only of the ones I care for."

"Why didn't we see any inhabitants from the other

realms?" Rikar asked, his gaze moving all around them as they moved past the city into a more rural setting. The crystal landscape remained, though tall buildings and streetlights had vanished, replaced by open fields, trees, and modest hut-like dwellings.

"The path was moving too quickly," Herman replied as he stepped off the path and moved towards a small village where they could see plenty of crystal livestock moving around. "You could see the landscapes except for the towns and villages where the people lived in."

"Why not?" Rikar frowned at him.

"There was no need for that, you didn't need to speak to anyone from there." Herman stopped beside one of the crystal huts and nodded ahead. "The last mystic from Leva will be over that hill." With those words he turned away and ambled towards a bench and sat down. When they stood there staring at him, he raised a brow. "Your time is running out; do you want to talk to him or not?"

"Aren't you going with us?" Calista asked him.

He shook his head. "Nope, I did my part. I showed you the way, the rest is up to you." He leaned back and sighed. "I would hurry if I were you."

Calista nodded and then they all moved swiftly past the huts and over the hill that Herman had gestured towards. When they reached the top, they saw several people who were tending to animals and one male who was laying down using a crystal hay pile as a pillow.

"Is that a piece of wheat in his mouth?" Eon looked at Calista, his brow crinkled.

She chuckled and shrugged. "I guess even with a world completely different from ours, there will always be similarities." She moved forward towards the nearest male that was tossing some crystal pellets into a pen where crystal feathers flew into the air from the chickens running for their food. "Hello, can you help us please?"

The male looked sideways at her, not pausing in his work as he spoke, "that depends."

"On what?" she asked him slowly.

"On what you need help with." The man shrugged his greenish colored shoulders and tossed more pellets into the pen.

"We're looking for someone named Minnow." Calista watched the man, but he continued to toss pellets into the pen, saying nothing. "Do you know this person?" When he still didn't say anything, she started to speak with more volume in case he didn't hear her, "We're looking for someone named Minnow."

"He can hear you," the male that lay on the ground drawled lazily, still chewing on the wheat stalk, staring straight ahead towards the mountains in the distance.

"So, why isn't he answering us?" Rikar growled.

"Because he isn't Minnow." The man played with the stalk in his mouth, rolling it with his tongue.

"Do you know who Minnow is?" Sav asked him.

"Depends." The stalk moved from one side of the man's mouth to the other.

"On what?" Calista sighed.

"On who's asking," the man replied, though he still hadn't even looked their way.

"Gaia sent us." Sav crossed her arms and looked down at the man. When he didn't respond she leaned down to look in his face. "Did you hear me?"

The man still stared towards the mountains, not even glancing their way while Sav attempted to move into his line of sight. "I heard you, but you still haven't answered my question," the man drawled, ignoring her attempts to garner his attention.

Sav jerked back up with a disgruntled look and shot Kaine a glare when he chuckled. Kaine held up his hands but still smiled. "Can't blame me for finding amusement in you getting some of your own attitude thrown back at you." Sav's eyes narrowed even more, but Kaine still smiled. Even Calista had to admit that he had a point, though she wasn't about to point that out to Sav.

Calista moved forward, carefully placing herself between Kaine and Sav before their discussion got any further. She looked down at the guy on the ground and held out her hand. "My name is Calista, I'm the Atlantean Goddess of Manipulation sent here by Gaia to locate the last mystic of Leva."

The man's gaze finally moved from the mountains to look at her outstretched hand with a quizzical look.

"It's a form of greeting, shaking one's hand." Calista attempted to explain, but when the guy continued to stare at her hand silently, she let it drop awkwardly.

"What do you want with the last mystic of Leva?" he asked her.

"We need his help in stopping the queen," Calista paused, remembering Herman's words about there being no queen here. "I mean in finding Leva, we're hoping that he can help us."

This time the man turned his full silver eyes onto her, they looked mesmerizing in his face of purple hues. "Calista?" He watched as she nodded, but stayed where she stood. He tossed the crystal wheat stalk and stood up to stare down at her. "Look no further." He grinned at her and held out his hand. "Minnow's the name."

Calista hesitated for several seconds before she finally gripped his hand in hers and gave a slight shake.

"Why couldn't you tell us that you were who we were looking for before?" Rikar growled at him, but the man lifted a shoulder and moved to lean against the nearby fence. "So, how do we find her?" Rikar asked him with another growl.

"You must be Rikar." Minnow's voice was calm, too calm in the face of Rikar's aggression. He regarded Rikar with the same unbothered interest Calista had seen the Ancients use when they wanted control without effort.

Rikar frowned and stepped closer. "How do you know my name?"

Minnow tilted his head, as if he was considering whether or not to respond. "Draken speaks of you often. Though he always claimed you were the lighthearted one." A faint smile touched Minnow's lips. "I'll have to correct him. Clearly, that was misinformation."

Rikar's whole body stiffened. "You talked to my brother?"

"Only when he passes through." Minnow's gaze drifted toward the distant mountains. "It's been some time, though. I'll send your regards when I see him again." Minnow turned back towards Calista, but Rikar grabbed at his shoulder and stopped him.

"Where is he?" Rikar demanded, following Minnow's earlier glance. His breath caught. "Draken..." Rikar released Minnow and broke into a run toward the mountains.

"Rikar!" Livinia shouted, already moving after him. Kaine and Eon followed without hesitation, Sav close behind.

"What in the dead realms is going on now?" Herman's voice boomed as he trudged down the slope, scowling after the fleeing group. His gaze snapped to Calista. "Where are they going?"

She shrugged helplessly.

"Damn the living," Herman muttered, vanishing in a shimmer of light as he stormed after them.

Calista sighed. "I better go and get them." She started to walk away but Minnow grabbed her arm.

"Please don't," he said softly. "I'd hate to think I caused all that trouble just for you to ruin the diversion."

She turned to look at him, her mouth going slack at his words. "You created that diversion?" she asked. When he nodded, she groaned and pressed her fingers to her brow. "Rikar is going to be really ticked off."

"We only have moments," Minnow said, his tone sharpening. "Before Herman expels you from Aetherfall. If you want to stop Leva, you need to listen to me."

Her head snapped up. "You know how?"

"I know why you were really sent here." He held her gaze. "What I'm about to tell you, you can't repeat."

Her jaw tightened. "That's not how this works. I was sent to gather information. I can't use what I can't share."

"Be careful who you share it with," Minnow said quietly, "or you'll never find the mystic."

She finally found her voice. "You're not the mystic?" she asked.

Minnow shook his head. "Nope."

"Then where is he?"

"Still hiding." His voice lowered. "And for good reason."

She folded her arms. "Minnow, stop circling the questions, I want answers."

"You weren't sent here to learn how to defeat Leva," he said. "They wanted to know if the mystic was truly here, in the land of the dead."

Calista frowned. "So, they don't know?"

"No, but I need you to make sure that they believe he is here," Minnow told her.

"How can I do that?" She felt confused. Nothing was making sense.

"By telling them that the mystic told you that you needed to gather certain components to locate Leva." He looked around them as he spoke. "Something only the true mystic should know."

"Which is?" She frowned.

"Essences," Minnow spoke as if that answered everything.

She frowned at him. "Essences of what?"

Minnow nodded. "Jaru. Ara. Gaia. Three signatures bound to her creation. Without all three, Leva cannot be found, only felt." He reached for the necklace that Grint had given her when she left Ara, but jerked back when Scratch reached out to swat at him for daring to get too close to his mistress. "You have a guardian hidden beneath those golden waves."

Calista smiled and leaned her head to touch her cheek to Scratch who disappeared beneath her hair once again.

Minnow laughed and nodded to the bauble around her neck. "You already have the essence of Ara in that vial around your neck. Now you just need the others."

Calista frowned and sighed. "So, Gaia already knew that we needed the essences to find her sister?"

Minnow nodded and Calista groaned. “How could they not know that the mystic wasn’t here?” she asked, trying to fight the confusion that felt as if it was drowning her.

“Because Gaia and Ara cannot enter Aetherfall,” Minnow replied. “So, they sent you in to see if the Mystic was indeed dead, or if he was alive and able to spill their secrets.”

“Secrets?” Calista frowned.

“Yes.” Minnow’s gaze darkened. “He knows their secrets. All of them. Truths they buried when their sister went after their brother. Truths they cannot afford to reveal.”

Calista swallowed. “So, they sent us to confirm his death.”

“Yes,” Minnow said. “And to know what he would say. If they believed that you knew those secrets, they would make you permanent residents here.”

Silence stretched between them.

“What do you want me to tell them?” she finally asked.

Minnow placed a small vial into her palm. The liquid inside shimmered faintly, as though it was yearning to be released.

“Tell them you met the mystic,” he said. “That he told you to gather the three essences to locate the queen. Tell them he spoke nothing else.”

Calista’s fingers closed around the vial. “And this?”

"Keep it hidden," Minnow replied. "Tuck it away where no one thinks to look, and speak of it to no one until the moment demands it. Some paths are not meant to be known until they are already walked." His gaze sharpened, meaning settling behind his words. "Not everyone who sent you would welcome what lies at the end of this one."

Her breath caught. "What am I meant to do with it?"

"When the time comes," Minnow said, stepping back, "offer it to your ship, not as fuel or command, but as a light meant only to be followed. Do not command it. Trust it. The path will reveal itself only to those who do not force it."

"But, how will I know when the time has come?" Calista frowned at him.

Minnow grinned at her. "The vial will let you know, there will be no doubt."

Before she could respond, Herman's furious voice echoed across the realm.

"You were warned not to wander!" he roared. The air ignited in blinding light. "Now get out of my realm!"

Minnow winked before he vanished from her sight.

CHAPTER 15

Light twisted, water screamed, and the portal collapsed inward and then exploded outward, flinging them from Aetherfall like unwanted debris. Calista felt the shove before she heard it, a brutal, unseen force driving her forward as Herman's voice echoed in their ears.

"Enough!"

She hit stone hard. Breath tore from her lungs as she skidded across the grotto floor, limbs tangled with Rikar, Livinia, Eon, Kaine, and Sav in a chaotic heap. Her ears rang and her chest burned. Scratch dug in, his tiny claws tight against her shoulder as water and fading light splashed and evaporated around them, leaving silence behind.

Gaia stood there waiting and watching. Roots curled upward from the ground around her feet while she stared at them calmly, too calmly, and heavier than the impact that had thrown them there.

Sav forced herself upright, jaw tight, fury cutting through her words as she snapped at them. "Seriously?" She glared at them. "You knew the rules and you still tried to break them?"

Calista dusted off her clothes, breathing in deeply as she tried not to snap. Her hand moving absently to soothe Scratch whose body was still tense. She looked at Sav, her eyes narrowed. "Tell me you would do something different if it was the chance to see someone you care about?"

The caustic remark they expected didn't come, instead Sav sighed and nodded. "I would've."

"Did you find out what you went to learn?" Gaia asked them.

The words were calm, but the Grotto tightened around them. Roots creaked beneath the stone. The air grew heavy, as if the world itself leaned closer to listen.

"Hey, we're okay, thanks for asking." Rikar glowered at her while he pushed himself up from the floor. Both Kaine and Eon wore the same disgruntled look on their faces.

Gaia didn't even look their way when she answered, her eyes focused on Calista. "I can see that you survived," Gaia said evenly. "That was not my question."

Calista swallowed, forcing her expression into something neutral, something careless. Scratch remained still against her shoulder, an anchor. "In a way," she said.

The silence that followed her words felt deliberate and almost dangerous. Rikar, Livinia, Kaine, and Eon moved closer to her, as if letting her know that they had her back. Something she prayed wouldn't be needed. Not against this goddess.

"Explain." Only one word but that one word had a lot of weight to it. Gaia's gaze felt as if they were standing there with an interrogation lamp pointed at them. Gave Calista a new appreciation for the suspects that her partners and herself would question.

Calista chose her words carefully, keeping her expression neutral as she did. Minnow's warning echoing in the back of her mind. "He told us that we needed the essence of you, Jaru, and Ara to locate her." She stood there stoically, reminding herself that she wasn't lying, she just wasn't elaborating. That way, Gaia couldn't feel any deception from her.

Gaia seemed to study her, really study her with eyes that were ancient and knowing. "Is that all that he told you?"

Calista took a deep breath, knowing she would have to answer carefully, lest Gaia detected deception from her. Something that could be a death sentence for them all. "Should there have been more?" For a few moments Calista expected Gaia to challenge her words, but instead Gaia gave a shake of her head.

"No," Gaia spoke softly. "There should not." She turned from Calista and nodded to Sav, as if the matter had been settled. As if there wasn't an unspoken truth that hung between them, heavy and alive.

Sav removed the globe from her staff and handed it to Calista. "Essence of Gaia." Calista looked into the globe where the sands were shining brightly and pulsing with ancient power.

Calista nodded as she took the globe with one hand and grasped the vial around her neck with the other. "And I have the essence of Ara, now we just need to find the essence of Jaru." She looked at Gaia. "Any idea on how we can do that?"

"I can help with that." Sav spoke up.

Calista turned to her slowly. "You can tell us where it is?"

"No." Calista's jaw tightened at her words. "But I can take you to it."

"Absolutely not!" Rikar growled, moving forward as his eyes burned with dragon fire. "You're not going."

Sav's lips curved, faint and knowing. "Then good luck finding Jaru's essence."

Silence stretched as Calista weighed her options. Minnow's warnings, Gaia's influence, the risk of bringing a devoted follower of Gaia into their ranks. Every instinct told her not to trust Sav, but they were out of options.

"Fine, you can come with us," Calista told her.

Rikar whirled towards her with a frown. "Calista..."

She held up a hand, cutting him off. Her eyes never left Sav. "But understand this, if you lie, if you lead us astray, or if I so much as suspect a hint of betrayal from you, I will personally see to it that you're ejected into the void of space."

Sav snorted. "If you think you can do it."

Rikar's growl was low and dangerous, but Calista

only shook her head. "We're done debating. Time is running out."

She turned away from them, already shimmering as her form dissolved into light. "We leave soon." Atlantis awaited with goodbyes she wasn't ready to say.

The shimmer faded, and Atlantis stood before them all in pale blue light under the waves. Calista breathed in deep and started forward only to be pulled to the side by Rikar who stared at her with eyes full of so much emotion.

"You're really going to let her come?" He nodded towards where Sav was already walking away from them and towards Atlantis. "A servant of Gaia? After everything that has happened?"

"We don't have a choice," Calista replied. "You know that."

"Doesn't mean I have to like it," Rikar growled watching Sav walking away.

"I know I don't." Calista stared at the retreating Sav as well. "Only thing we can do is keep an eye on her and if she goes to betray us then we follow through on our threat."

"Gladly." Rikar flexed his fists at his side starting towards Atlantis.

"Herman was right," Calista said, her voice sad.

Rikar frowned and looked back. "About what?"

"You used to be so carefree." Calista sighed. "I miss that Rikar."

"And I miss my brother." Rikar glared before he turned and walked away.

"You had to say that, didn't you?" Livinia looked at her.

Calista nodded and sighed. "I did."

Eon grabbed her hand and gave a comforting squeeze. "Let's go say goodbye, sis." Calista nodded and let him lead her forward.

Malis met them as soon as they entered the city. She pulled Calista into her arms first, fierce and grounding, then drew Eon in with them. Cael followed, his arms wrapped around them all, his forehead against Calista's as he held tightly.

When they drew apart Malis looked at them both and spoke with an unyielding tone, "you will come back, both of you. No exceptions." Her eyes shined with unshed tears but she wouldn't let them go until they both nodded.

Tylaos and Malov stepped forward, their presence ancient and calm. Tylaos held them both to him as Malov placed gentle kisses to their foreheads. "I second your mother's decree." Tylaos smiled at them both. "No exceptions." They nodded and then said goodbye to the others who were gathered in quiet solidarity. Rowena, Lison, Vesper, Vapor and Brine all smiled at them, hugging them and making them promise to come home.

Stratos and Atmos bowed to them as they moved

past to where Kaine stood apart from all, his arms crossed with John and Allen flanking him. The time for goodbyes had passed, it was time to board their ship and head back to the stars.

CHAPTER 16

Calista entered her cabin and placed both the essence of Ara and Gaia into a padded locker where she had no worries about them getting damaged. Scratch peered out at her from his position on her shoulder, his expression one of curiosity. "Just keeping them safe." She smiled at him and patted his head. "Now, we can head to the bridge and update the rest." With that, they moved from her cabin to the bridge where the others waited. She didn't want to tell the others anything until they were far enough from Earth, but she could wait no longer.

"Where are we going?" Rikar asked her as soon as she entered the bridge. His gruff manner had become so much like his brother that it made Calista's heart hurt.

"To find the mystic." Calista strode to the view screen, looking out at the dark space around them. The silence on the bridge was deafening, but it was Sav's reaction that Calista watched closely from the corner of her eye. Her expression turned to surprise as she looked at Calista, her mouth slightly agape, though she stayed silent. The others had no problem voicing their amazement.

“The mystic?” Her brother frowned at her. “Minnow wasn’t-“

“No,” Calista said, sharper than she meant to. “He was just a…” Calista paused as she tried to come up with the right words.

“A decoy,” Rikar muttered.

Calista nodded. “Yes, that’s what he was.” She turned away from the view screen. “A shield because whoever hid the mystic believed the Empyreans would kill him if they knew he still lived.”

“How can he still be alive?” Kaine asked. “Mystics aren’t immortal, they have a stronger connection to their empyrean which makes their lifeforce stronger than most, but if he no longer has any connection to his empyrean, how could he live so long? This doesn’t make sense.”

“I don’t have any answers to those questions,” Calista admitted. “I wish I did. I can only assume that either the rules changed, or someone broke them.” She gave a slight shrug of her shoulders.

“We can ask the Mystic when we find him.” Rikar cracked his knuckle by linking his fingers and stretching out. Livinia looked over at him with a slight grin on her face.

“And you’re certain he’s alive?” Sav asked, watching Calista closely.

Calista turned to meet her gaze and hold it. “I’m certain enough to act.”

Stryx scoffed. "Act how? We don't have any coordinates, or a trail, do we? Any breadcrumbs laying around for us to follow?"

Calista chuckled silently. Lissy was always quizzing the crew on Earth sayings, they didn't always get them right, but sometimes they did manage pretty well.

"No breadcrumbs," she admitted and reached to pet Scratch, who nuzzled her hand before covertly sliding the vial that Minnow had given her into her loose grip. The vial felt warm between her fingers, as if it had been waiting for her. "But Minnow didn't leave me empty-handed either."

Calista crossed to the navigation console, her stride confident and sure, though she didn't feel it on the inside. She couldn't explain it, but somehow, she knew that she was doing the right thing. Minnow gave no instructions, just that the vial would know.

"Calista, what're you doing?" Rikar frowned as she stood in front of the console.

"Listening," she responded as she uncorked the vial in her hand.

"What is that?" Kaine frowned.

Calista tilted the vial and let the fine, luminous dust fall across the console's surface. "I guess you could call it our breadcrumbs." She gave a half smile as the console started to glow softly and the ship shuddered.

"Whoa!" Clyde had reached to adjust a setting on the navigation console when he got tossed back, the console glowing as if to reprimand him. He glared up at her. "What gives?"

"I don't know." Calista shook her head and lifted her shoulders.

"Seems, the ship is flying itself and doesn't want our help," Clori said as she moved back from her controls as well. She looked over at Stryx. "I don't think we're in control anymore."

Stryx's expression darkened as he turned to Calista. "I hope you know what you're doing, because right now, we're hostages to that powder of yours."

Calista sighed and walked out. "Me too," she spoke softly as she exited the bridge. She needed to gather her thoughts and honestly, there wasn't anything she could do on the bridge. She had already given complete control to a glowing powder, now she just prayed that she did the right thing.

Calista walked into the small dining room and pulled down a mug to fill it with steaming hot water. She sprinkled some of the energy herbs that Bastion grew into the water, watched as the herbs dissipated into the water, creating Zazzy juice. Holding the mug in both her hands she took a deep sip of the juice. She sat in her favorite plush chair with her mug when the door swished open for Rikar, Livinia, Kaine, Eon, and Sav to enter with John and Allen following.

She knew the discussion on the bridge wasn't over,

she just wished she had more to tell them. It wasn't like Minnow was a wealth of information.

"You should've told us sooner," Rikar told her as he sat down on a table and used a nearby chair for a foot stool. Livinia stayed by the door while Eon, Kaine, John and Allen all took seats in chairs and couches in the small dining room. Calista was beginning to think she might have been better off going to the mess hall.

Sav leaned against the wall closest to the door, though she said nothing, just watched Calista.

"I told you when it was safe," Calista replied evenly. "Minnow didn't want me to say anything that the Empyreans could overhear. I needed to be careful."

Sav tilted her head, looking right at Calista. "And you think space makes us deaf to the gods?"

"No," Calista acknowledged. "I think it makes them slower, which gives us a head start."

The others looked at each other silently, their expressions unreadable.

"I won't pretend I know everything," Calista continued. "But I won't lie to you either. The mystic was hidden because someone believed the Empyreans would destroy him. And if that's true…" She let that thought hang in the air.

"Then this isn't just a search," Livinia pondered.

"No," Calista said softly. "It's a risk." Her gaze flicked to Sav, who was watching her closely. "And one I intend to survive." The challenge was clear, though Sav looked unfazed as she stared back.

Calista moved about the ship, Scratch peering out from beneath her hair. It had been many days since she sprinkled the dust on the console, which made Stryx, Clyde, and Clare irrelevant to the ship's functions. Something they made sure to mention often. With no clear path of where they were going, and too much time on their hands, the crew had been getting edgy. Not that Calista could blame any of them, she was feeling a tad touchy herself.

She smiled when she saw the sign on the cargo bay door; the one Bastion had claimed for his arboretum.

Authorized personnel only!

Allen had attempted to bring everyone's spirit up, so he snuck into the arboretum and snagged some herbs for cooking. He figured all the herbs in the arboretum were for cooking, except some were medicinal, and then you have the ones that were used to create good smells. Those weren't the best for eating, but those were the ones that Allen picked to put into the stew he made.

It smelled great, although the taste had Stryx, Vester and Allen himself sick for a few days. Most of the others were either put off by the smell, or just got to dinner late, like Calista, thankfully. They were the lucky ones. Allen has since been barred from both the arboretum and the kitchen.

She moved further down the corridor and heard the grunting sound of Kaine and Rikar sparring in the training bay. She peeked in to see Kaine end up on his back, though he was quick to recover and move swiftly out of the way. Rikar landed right where Kaine had been only moments before. They were both sweating but at least they were being friendly, as they sparred with one another.

Since the ship had been on auto pilot to only the dust knows where, everyone had too much time on their hands. With no set destination, no new Ancient prison they were going to infiltrate, they all had to find ways to keep their minds busy. Kaine and Rikar had slowly come to terms with one another; though no words were spoken, they found other means of communication. Calista would never understand how males think, though she was just glad they were starting to get along.

She moved past the training bay and made a left turn, descended down a flight of stairs to a lower deck. Scratch peered out then quickly went back to his hiding spot. Since Solen had given him life once again, he barely left her shoulder, and if he did, he made sure to never wander too far. Except for in Atlantis, when he went off and explored the home he barely got to know, before the Ancients had attempted to end his life.

The musical melody from Cellica's room drifted down the hallway. During this downtime, Cellica had been teaching some of the crew dancing, Livinia had become her favorite student. During the first class, every one ended up on their ass several times, except for Livinia. She did it perfectly and Cellica proudly proclaimed with a laugh, "of course you did."

Turning another corner, she paused as she saw John and Sav speaking in a nearby alcove, while she wasn't one to eavesdrop, she stayed where she was. Since that day at Stahle's bar, those two usually stayed away from one another. So, just to make sure she was there to intervene in case things got heated, or that was what she told herself, she stayed there. Had nothing to do with curiosity at all.

"You weren't trying to flirt with my girlfriend, back on Earth, were you?" Sav asked him while he played with some stabilizer parts in his massive hands. He had been helping Bern with some maintenance in engineering.

John looked down at the parts, rotating them within one of his hands. He said nothing though his massive figure deflated just a bit. Calista was prepared to intervene if Sav did anything to hurt John. He might not be the smartest crew member, but he had the biggest heart and always tried the hardest. If not for Kaine and Allen, he might have been friendless on the ship. Most of everyone on the ship, Calista included, had been more worried about their objective than making friends with their new crewmates.

She felt a tinge of guilt, but she pushed that down as she waited to see if John would answer. He did not.

"You were rehearsing." Sav observed. Calista frowned, unsure of what Sav was talking about.

John gave a shuddering sigh. "Yeah," he admitted heavily, the parts rolling from his hands onto the table between them. "I didn't mean to be disrespectful; I just wanted it to be perfect when I finally got up the nerve to ask her out."

Calista frowned, unsure of who John could be speaking about.

Sav placed her hand on top of John's. "That's your problem." John looked up at her with a frown, but she continued. "Cellica doesn't seem like someone who needs perfection." John looked back down at his hands and Sav smiled at him. "Besides, I heard she was really impressed by whomever it was that fixed the dancefloor in her room. She said those reinforcements made her dancefloor sturdier. Seems, she has inquired about who had done such a wonderful deed, but no one came forward."

Calista's mouth went slack at what she heard. She had no idea that John had a thing for Cellica, though to be honest, it wasn't like she paid much attention to anything other than their next objective. She moved quietly away, not wanting either one to know she had been there. She turned a different corner and headed back to the small dining room.

On the way she saw Vestor sitting with Eon and Allen in the mess hall. Vestor had attempted a few times to tell one of Ara's folk tales, but usually ended with a sigh, saying, "my sister tells it better." Calista remembered Velva, the barb of Ara, as very soft spoken and would sing a song so powerful it could bring tears to the coldest of hearts. Eon listened while tossing a cup in the air, freezing time so that it stayed there for a few moments before he restarted time again.

Calista ended her journey in the small dining room that she had taken as her own, mainly because the others preferred their rooms or the larger mess hall that had more options than this small room. She grabbed a mug and filled it with Zazzy juice, before she sat in her favorite chair staring out into the space outside the view port. She sighed. "I miss you, Solen."

CHAPTER 17

The stars flew by the ship, at least that was how it looked to Calista, while she sat in her favorite chair staring out the view port. The sound of Scratch softly snoring in her ear, and the feel of his soft breathing on her neck, soothed the tension in her body. The warm mug in her hand helped as well, Bastion had brought her some new herbs from his arboretum when she ran out. He always made sure she was taken care of, told her that he promised Solen he would look after her.

It had been weeks now, since the ship had been on auto pilot, with the dust as the new navigator. Stryx, Clyde, and Clare all had asked her when they would reach their destination and get the control of their ship back.

She had no answer for them.

This idleness had been hard on her as well, she wasn't even sure exactly how long it had been since that day. The days all seemed to meld into one, you couldn't tell one apart from the other. They were moving through the stars with no sense of direction, the dust rendering all navigation, communication, and flight systems useless.

Calista had no idea what the queen was planning and no way to contact anyone beyond the ship. If the Ancients decided to attack, they would never see it until it was too late.

The unknowing was worse than an all-out battle. She sighed as she leaned her head back and stared up at the ceiling. How she was ready for something to happen, anything.

"Hey Cali."

Calista turned to see Allen standing there, watching her. She nodded in greeting to him, but said nothing. She had too much going on in her head to even know what to say.

"Can I ask you about your time in Aetherfall?" he asked and she nodded, turning her chair to face him as well. "Kaine said that it was the Empyreans land of the dead, that all the dead would be there." She nodded though she knew that it was only the dead of those who were true children of the Empyreans, she didn't want to interrupt him with that knowledge, so she stayed silent and waited. "Did you see him?"

She didn't ask who he meant, she knew. Her throat tightened as she thought about Solen. She gave a slow shake of her head.

"I'm glad I didn't go," Alan admitted. "I don't think I could've left without looking for him."

"I truly wanted to, but I knew that if I did, I would lose the only chance we had of defeating the queen,"

Calista sighed and admitted. "No, I knew if I found him that I wouldn't have been able to leave there." Her voice broke. "He asked me to live and to defeat the queen, I promised him I would. I couldn't break that promise."

"So, do you think that we have the answer on how to defeat her?" Allen asked, attempting to change the subject.

Calista gave a humorless chuckle. "Not sure if you would say we have the answer, but we at least have a direction to go."

"How helpful is that?" Allen asked her.

"Not very." Calista's lips curled into a wry grin. "But something is better than nothing." She stood up and placed her mug on the nearest table before she turned to Allen. "We'll avenge your brother, that I promise."

"Can you do that without losing yourself?" he asked her, bringing a frown to her face. "My brother wouldn't want you to waste your life on vengeance. He would want you to live."

"I'm not wasting my life, and I refuse to let others suffer as we have." Calista swallowed hard. "I'm finishing what your brother started."

"Just don't lose yourself along the way." Allen gave her a small smile and then left the room. The door quietly closed behind him.

Calista turned to look out the window at the passing stars, breathing in deeply while she thought about Allen's words. She understood his concern, but she couldn't stop, not until the queen was defeated and the Ancients no longer a threat. She turned to walk out the same door that Allen left moments before. Moving down the corridors that she had wandered almost daily while waiting for something, anything to happen.

"Calista, to the bridge!"

Stryx's voice sounded urgent over the ship wide com. Calista started towards the bridge quickly, not sure what she was going to find. She did say that she wanted something to happen.

The glow from the bridge could be seen down the hallway before Calista even entered. The glow was even brighter when she entered, the console where she sprinkled the dust was so bright that it almost engulfed the whole bridge.

"Is this what is supposed to happen?" Stryx asked her.

Calista gave a slow shake of her head. "I don't know, it was supposed to guide us to the mystic." She looked at the view screen but saw nothing. She turned to Stryx. "Is there anything out there?"

He snorted. "Not that I can see." He then gestured towards the console and other blinking lights around the bridge. "Not that any of our sensors can pick up, the only fricken thing going off is that stupid dust that is almost blinding," he grumbled as he kept pushing buttons while Clori wore the same bewildered look as she moved from console to console.

"It would be nice to know what is going on?" She groused as her hand slammed against one of the wall consoles. "This stupid—" She stopped mid-sentence and turned to Stryx with wide eyes.

Calista felt the ship slowing down until it felt as if it was no longer moving. She turned to look at both Stryx and Clori, who both looked stunned. "Why did you guys stop?"

"We didn't," Clori answered slowly. The ship rumbled and they could hear the sound of gears grinding. "Nor did we start the landing operation."

"We're landing?" Kaine entered with Rikar, Livinia, Sav, and Eon.

Stryx shrugged and started moving from console to console, avoiding the main glowing one. "It seems so, although I didn't give the order." His gruff words sounded alarmed.

"Then who did?" Rikar frowned.

Stryx motioned towards the glowing console that no one could get near without being blinded. "Ask our bodiless navigator, it doesn't seem to want to be very informative. It's taken away our ability to pilot the ship and even know where the heck we're going. Now, it's landing on its own without us being able to do anything about it." The aggravation in Stryx's tone was very obvious.

"Where are we landing?" Kaine asked as he moved further into the room, peering into the dark view screen where only darkness stared back at him.

"Again," Stryx spoke through tight lips. "Ask our glowing navigator."

Everyone went still when they felt the jolt as the ship touched down on something solid. "Wherever we are, I guess we're here," Eon said as he moved to leave the bridge. "No sense standing here and growling at each other over something we can't control, let's go see where we are."

Kaine smirked before he followed. "Kid has a point."

They exited the ship, unsure of what they would find, and stepped out onto a world full of life. Trees, bushes and flowers all abloom, teeming with vibrancy. Birdlike creatures flying around with wings that looked like the hummingbirds back home, except that the wings were moving in a circular motion around the head of the bird, keeping them afloat. Furry creatures with big eyes, small bodies but large paws lumbered between the bushes.

"Where are we?" Eon walked while he looked around him at all the colorful flora there was to see, and amazing fauna that scuttled around. "This doesn't look like Earth nor any of the other planets that we've been to."

"It kind of looks like a combination of them all." Calista lifted one of the colorful leaves to breathe in the scent deeply.

"Good observation."

They all started at the crackly voice and looked around them to see where it came from.

"Where are you?" Kaine called out.

"Right behind you," came the answer.

They turned to see an Aggie standing on a fallen tree that created a bridge between two stumps. The same crystal skin, rainbow hair, and clothes that resembled the flora all around him.

"An Aggie?" Kaine breathed.

"Aggie?" Bastion appeared and jumped on Kaine's head who grunted. They hadn't realized that Bastion had joined the landing party, but then again, it took them a few months before they discovered that he had stowed away on their ship. "You look like Sanders." Bastion tilted his head and looked at the older Aggie.

"I'm his father, Gragers," the Aggie told them, though he didn't show the age of Sanders. His beard wasn't as long and his colors more vibrant. "I left Ara long ago, though I hadn't expected to be gone this long." The Aggie sighed.

"Why?" Bastion asked while the others watched.

"Oh, he's so sweet." Cellica appeared and knelt down before Gragers. "Hello, I'm Cellica. How're you?"

Gragers peered up at her. "You're weird," he told her.

"Hey!" John frowned down at the small Aggie who looked up with wide eyes. "You be nice to her!" He growled.

"You're a giant!" Gragers turned and jumped into a nearby bush and disappeared.

"Dammit!" Rikar growled and frowned at John who was already hanging his head. "We needed him, we don't know where we are and he might've been able to give us answers. You just had to scare him off." He growled.

"I'm sorry," John said with a sigh.

Rikar growled and started to walk away towards the very direction that Gragers had disappeared.

Cellica placed a gentle hand on John's arm and gave him a smile. "It's all right, John. I appreciate the effort." She kissed his cheek before she turned to follow Rikar.

John stared after her, his hand holding his cheek and his eyes following her with a lovestruck expression. Sav chuckled and patted John's shoulder. "Let's go big guy, you made some forward movement with her, don't ruin it." John gave a bemused nod and moved forward.

They all followed Rikar and Cellica along the path, looking around at the scenery they passed. Colorful trees that reminded them of Ara, animals almost like the ones at home although a bit different, and rivers that reminded them of Earth. So much life around them, from a planet that hadn't even shown up on their sensors.

"Does anyone even know what planet this is?" Allen asked as he looked down into the river they were walking by. There were shadows in the water that swam by.

"Considering it didn't even show up on the sensors, not really." Stryx grimaced. "This area hasn't seen much activity since Jaru was destroyed."

"That's for sure." A slow drawl had them turning to see a beefy male leaning against a colorful tree. He barely stood four feet tall, his dark hair curled around his face, matching the color of his beard and mustache. "Makes me wonder where all of you came from?"

"The better question is, who are you?" Rikar growled from behind him. Rikar reached for the guy but he disappeared, only to reappear crouching down on a tree stump with a grin. "What are you?" Rikar frowned.

"You invade my home and you dare to demand answers of me?" The male asked, tilting his head to the side as he stared at Rikar. "I think you have the whole situation backwards, you are the interlopers who need to explain themselves, not me."

"You'll have to excuse our friend." Calista moved to situate herself between the weird male and Rikar. "We're looking for the remaining mystic of Leva. I was given some dust that guided our ship here where it landed all on its own."

"Why are you looking for this mystic?" The male asked her, his expression full of curiosity.

"We need to defeat the queen and we need this mystic's help," Calista told him.

"What makes you think this mystic can help you defeat this queen?" The guy asked her.

"Minnow told us to seek out this mystic, that he would be able to help us," Calista said.

The male looked at her curiously. "Is that all he said?" he asked her.

Calista pursed her lips. "That's all that matters."

"Are you sure about that?" The guy grinned at her, pulling a frown from her. It was as if this guy knew about the whole conversation. But no one was there.

"What's he talking about Calista?" Rikar asked her, crossing his arms and staring at her.

Calista glared at the male and turned to stare at Rikar, crossing her own arms. "The only other thing that was told to me, I told all of you on the ship."

Rikar raised a brow. "Are you sure about that? Seems like it took a bit to pull that out of you, could there be something else you aren't telling us? Those of us who've left their home to help you, been there from day one, yet you don't seem to impart everything you know."

"I'm positive," Calista shot back. "And what do you mean that you've been by my side this whole time? The only reason you're here is to avenge Draken's death. Not to help me do anything," she threw back at him.

"And you're on the journey to avenge Solen's death," he told her, staring down at her while the others started to look nervous. "So, how does that make you any different?"

"I'm not lying about that, nor am I attempting to say that I'm here to help anyone out," Calista shot back, staring straight into his eyes as she let out some of the pain that she had been building up when it came to

Rikar. "You need to quit lying to yourself!" Her hands moved to her hips.

Rikar growled at her, his eyes shifting to dragon, though he kept himself from transforming completely. "I'm not lying to myself, though I also don't try to hide anything from my friends."

"We haven't been friends in a while, Rikar." Calista felt her throat tighten as she spoke. All the hurt and pain she had been pushing down rose to the surface. The others looked around, looking as if they would rather be anywhere but here at this moment. Livinia, Kaine, and Eon attempted to look as if they weren't listening, but their posture showed they were also ready to act if needed.

The sound of someone loudly clearing their throat turned all the attention from Calista and Rikar who were both breathing hard and glaring at one another. The husky male was still standing there. "I thought this was all about trying to save others from losing their freedom or their loved ones as you both have? This sounds way more personal to me. Sounds like neither of you have been truly honest with yourselves or each other."

CHAPTER 18

Calista frowned at the male. "You're awful knowledgeable." Her arms crossed as she turned from Rikar to look at the guy. "Especially for someone who doesn't know any of us. Nor were you there in Aetherfall when I spoke with Minnow."

The male watched her from his perch on the tree trunk, though from time to time his gaze flitted over to where Rikar glowered at him. "What is that you're attempting to imply? You still haven't admitted to what else Minnow told you."

She frowned at him as she debated whether to answer him or not, though the dust brought her to this destination, she worried whether it was a trick. She opened her mouth to answer him, then thought better of it. She closed her mouth and stared at the male who watched her with something akin to amusement. "How do I know I can trust you? What if you're just trying to get answers to harm the mystic?"

"Not bad." The male leapt off the trunk and walked around her with a grin before he held out his hand to her. "Lantis is the name."

She slowly reached out and took his hand, her expression still one of uncertainty. "Lantis? Is that your real name?" She wondered if he was just messing with her, giving her a made-up name that was close to the name of her home.

"You came all this way to see me and then make fun of my name?" Lantis frowned at her.

"You're the mystic?" Eon asked the guy as Calista stared in shock. This man didn't feel like a mystic to her, but then again, the only types of people she met from Leva were the Ancients. She didn't have much to go on.

Lantis chuckled, "that would be something all right." They frowned at him. "Our people live a long time but not that long. I'm not the mystic, but I am a descendant of his."

Calista looked over at the others, not too sure how to proceed, this wasn't what she expected. "So, you can help us in defeating the queen?" Calista asked.

Lantis moved past them and slammed his hand on a nearby tree, laughing when Gragers fell out and landed on the ground with a thud. "There you are, old man. I knew you were hiding in that tree." Lantis laughed louder, his head held up high with pride.

Gragers lumbered to his feet and glared up at Lantis. "You keep playing your games and your father will have some words for you."

"Oh, don't be such a spoiler," Lantis chided with a grin as he skipped around Gragers. "You're just upset because I gave away your hiding spot so that you couldn't eavesdrop." He laughed even harder when Gragers pointed at him with his stubby finger.

"Lantis," Calista called out but he was too busy laughing to hear her. Rikar let out a dragon roar that shook the world around them. Lantis covered his ears with his hands and frowned at Rikar who was glaring back at him. "We need to talk to you," she told him but Lantis was still giving Rikar dirty looks. "Lantis." Calista once again attempted to get his attention.

He turned to her, his lips pressed together before he crossed his arms. "I've changed my mind; I'm not helping you." With that, he disappeared.

Calista stood there, her mouth open but no words came out. She wasn't sure what to say as she didn't understand what had happened. They needed the mystic to tell them how to defeat the queen, but he was acting awfully erratic. She turned to see the same mystified expression mirrored back from her by the others who were attempting to process what had happened as well.

"I wouldn't worry about Lantis," Grager told them as he reached down and picked up a wooden stick that he proceeded to use to clean out his ears. "The big oaf's roar just upset his frail feelings, is all."

"But, how will we defeat the queen without his help?" Calista asked, not sure if she was asking Grager or if she was just asking to ask.

"He can't help you," Grager told her, still using the stick to clean out his ears.

"What do you mean? He's the mystic." Kaine frowned at Grager.

"Nah, he's not the mystic," Grager told them before he pitched the stick into the forest. "At least, not yet."

"So, who is the mystic then?" Eon asked, unsure if they would even get an answer.

Grager opened his mouth to say something, then his gaze moved past them and his eyes widened while his mouth shut.

"Grager." They turned to see another male standing there. This one was taller than Lantis and more slender. His hair wasn't as dark, though it was longer. Grager gave a small bow towards the male, then moved back to stand close to the trees. The male turned towards them and gave them a slight nod. "You'll have to excuse Lantis, he tends to get a tad excited around strangers, we don't get many visitors here."

"When's the last time you had visitors?" Kaine asked him.

The male tilted his head; his forehead crinkled as his gaze turned thoughtful. "I'm not sure I can even remember the last time we had visitors."

Grager cleared his throat.

The male's face started to clear. "I think you're right G, the last time we had visitors was when your ship crashed here." He gave a small chuckle. "Been a long time, my friend." Grager smiled and nodded.

"Who are you?" Calista asked him.

"I'm sorry," the male apologized and held out his

hand. "My name is Eryx." Calista took his hand and gave it a shake, watching his face carefully.

"Such a pretty tattoo." Cellica tilted her head as she stared at the tattoo wrap around his forearm.

"Calista." Eon pointed to the tattoo, pulling Calista's attention from Eryx's face.

Her eyes widened at what she saw. A band of thorns woven intricately, creating a crown and in the center, she could make out the letters C and T. The C and T were connected together as if they made up a single letter.

She looked at him and he grinned. "My family's crest," he told her.

"You're the mystic," she breathed.

"Guilty as charged," he said, his smile turning rueful.

"Lantis is a descendant of yours?" Calista asked him with a frown.

"You could say that," Eryx said with a grin. "He's my son." Then he gave a sigh. "You'll have to excuse him. He was just trying to protect me in his own way." Another sigh. "His thoughts tend to wander without warning, but they usually return with something wonderous." He gave a wry smile.

"One thing I don't understand." Kaine approached him cautiously.

Eryx looked over at him and nodded. "Yes?"

"How are you still alive?" Kaine held out his hands that shook slightly. "It's been many lifetimes since the queen had destroyed Jaru. You've been separated from your Empyrean since then. How could you survive?" Kaine's expression was one of someone trying to understand something that seemed unattainable.

"Good genes!" Eryx suggested with a slight grin.

Rikar moved forward, his fists clenched at his side. "I don't care how you've managed to stay alive; we were told you could help us defeat the queen. Can you? Or are you telling us that we just wasted our time, once again?" He growled.

Eryx turned towards him, tilted his head and grinned. "Are you always this pleasant?"

Calista sighed when she saw the widening of Rikar's eyes, she moved forward before his eyes could completely turn dragon, hoping she could descale the situation. "We're all tired of getting jerked around only to find we've been chasing a dead end." She tried to explain to Eryx, though his eyes were still watching Rikar.

Rikar turned on her and frowned. "I don't need you standing up for me, I mean what I said, and I can back what I say myself."

Calista turned to stare at him, keeping her arms loosely at her side, trying to not be confrontational. Something that wasn't easy for her, when confronted, she usually turns confrontational herself. But they finally found the mystic, she didn't want to frighten him off, she wanted to learn how to stop the queen so they could finish this. She just wanted this all to end, no matter what the end was.

"I'm not defending you," she told him. "I'm just stating facts." She gave a loose shrug.

"Lantis may shift his attentions erratically, but he was right about the harmony of this familial unit being off," Eryx said softly, though his tone carried and caught the attention of all. "This family shouldn't be at each other's throats like this; you need to be in harmony if you want to defeat the queen."

"As she said, we're not friends and definitely not family." Rikar growled. "So, no problem. Not a familial unit."

"You're taking my words out of context." Calista turned to him, her hands going to her hips, forgetting about her earlier decision not to be confrontational.

"Really?" Rikar glared down at her. "Exactly how did you mean it when you said we aren't friends."

Calista breathed out hard. "What I said was that we haven't been friends in a while."

"And that's different how?" Rikar demanded as his skin started to shift in his agitation.

Calista stared up at him, she knew he could never hurt her physically, so that wasn't a worry. What she hated was the distance that had come to pass between them, when once they had been so close. She also hated that she didn't know how to fix it, or if she even could. She swallowed down a lump that formed in her throat and gave a helpless shrug. "Maybe it isn't."

"I'm very sad to hear that," Eryx said, his tone and expression looking sympathetic.

Calista swallowed again, attempting to swallow all the emotions that threatened to overwhelm her. She turned to Eryx, attempting to smile, while the others watched silently. "Can you please help us?" she asked him.

"I'm sorry, I can't," Eryx told them to their shock and dismay.

"But, Minnow told me that the dust would bring me to you, and that you could help us in defeating the queen," Calista said, her whole being feeling as if it had been sucker punched.

"I wish I could," Eryx said.

"So, why won't you?" Rikar growled at him.

Eryx turned to look at him, his expression calm and unreadable; utterly unaffected by the threat in Rikar's voice. "There needs to be harmony if you hope to defeat the queen," he said. "And there isn't." His gaze moved between them. "You're both so closed off from one another that you refuse to acknowledge there's even a problem. You act as if this is normal." Eryx shook his head. "It isn't."

Silence settled over the group. No one argued. No one met anyone else's eyes. The truth of his words hung there, heavy and undeniable. They had all seen it. Worse, they had all chosen to ignore it.

"What if we were able to talk out our problems?" Calista asked him. "Find a way to reach some kind of harmony between us?"

Eryx shook his head. "You two are too closed off to find harmony."

"But-"

He lifted a hand, stopping her. "You speak as if harmony is something you can force," he said, his voice firm but not unkind. He looked at her then, not in anger, but with the disappointment reserved for someone who should know better. "It isn't."

Eryx exhaled slowly. "I only hope it won't be too late when you finally understand what your stubbornness has cost you."

Calista looked at the others, guilt tightening in her chest, but her gaze always drifted back to Rikar. He stood rigid, fists clenched at his sides, offering nothing; no anger, no reassurance, no crack she could reach through.

They had followed her. Trusted her. And because of her stubbornness, they had lost time they could never reclaim, standing no closer to defeating the queen than when they began.

She searched for words anyway, for something that might mend what had fractured between them, but nothing came. She didn't know how to speak to him without making it worse, or whether the damage could be undone at all.

For the first time, the weight of it all settled fully on her shoulders. Not just the coming battle; but the quiet certainty that if the universe fell, it would be because she had led them here and still had no answers.

"We're going to help them."

CHAPTER 19

Turning around they saw a male most beautiful with multi-colored skin and long dark hair that sparkled like the view outside of the view screen on the ship. He was perfect in appearance and when he moved it was as if time itself stopped. Calista watched him, she couldn't pull her gaze away from the vision of this male.

"Jaru!" Sav bowed down, her arms outspread as her head touched the ground in front of her. Sav's words and actions pulled Calista out of her trance, she turned to frown at Sav and then her gaze moved back to the male that Sav just called Jaru.

Jaru lifted a hand, stilling her. "Rise. I no longer hold the power that commands such devotion. What I was has faded, and I have withdrawn from all that remains."

Sav rose slowly, her head bowed slightly before she turned to the others who stared at her in confusion. "I would say that I'm sorry to have deceived you, but that would be a lie. I am no child of Gaia, Ara, Leva, or even Jaru. I'm more than that."

"You've got to be kidding me!" Kaine exploded as he looked at everyone. "Has everyone gone mad? Has up become down and left become right? First, we find out the mystic of Leva is alive and well, then we find out Jaru is actually alive, and now?" He gave a sharp shake of his head. "Now, Sav isn't a child of our Empyreans but something more?" He looked at her. "What could be more? Are you an Empyrean?"

"No, still, I'm much more," she responded.

"What is more than that?" John asked her quietly.

"I'm part of a tribe that is able to live on any Empyrean of the Primordial, as if I were their child. They know not of my origin, only that I serve them." Sav said with a smile. "Gaia never knew, and I only truly stayed there because of my girlfriend. My quest was to find Jaru, and when I met you, I knew that you were the key." She gave a shrug. "I was right."

Allen plopped down on the ground. "This is just too much." He looked over at Bastion who was watching him. "Are you truly of Ara?"

Bastion snorted. "Of course, I am. I have no secrets," he declared as he sat next to Allen.

"Really?" Allen asked him. "How about all the murals of Calista in the-"

"Hush!" Bastion held his hand over Allen's mouth with a frown. He looked to the others. "He knows nothing of what he says." A few silent snickers and grins produced, but no one pushed any further. Calista didn't think she had ever seen an Aggie blush, but Bastion was doing a good job.

Calista turned to Sav. "Why were you looking for Jaru? And who is this Primordial that you mentioned?" She then turned to Eryx. "And why didn't you tell us that Jaru was still alive and that you were living on him?"

"Eryx was just trying to protect me," Jaru informed her, turning her attention away from Eryx and Sav. He then sighed. "He isn't living on me, this planet we stand on wasn't of my creation. If I had created it, then I would've been visible to my family."

"So, who created it then?" Calista frowned.

"He survived; we helped!" A female Aggie appeared next to Bastion and grinned proudly.

"Who's we?" Bastion asked her while peering at her with curiosity.

"All of us!" All around them Picknies appeared. Aggies, Karkens, Jinsons, and Carpes. Aggies from the trees, Carpes from the water while the Jinsons created icy film along the edges of the rivers, and Karkens sat upon piles of heated magma that just appeared.

The female Aggie with short spiky rainbow hair pointed towards Grager. "Our family joined forces to protect him before Leva made it here. We brought some of his essence here to revive him. Other Picknies wanted to help."

Calista turned to Eryx with a frown. "I thought you said that his spaceship crashed here, not that they created this world."

Eryx lifted his shoulder in a slight shrug. "I didn't

lie, I just omitted the fact that when he crashed, this was merely a meteorite that could barely sustain any life." Eryx sighed. "When I realized what was happening on Leva, saw the premonition of what she had done, I sent word to the mystic on Jaru and fled Leva."

Eryx paused and looked around them. "My ship crashed here and I ended up with a front row seat to the destruction of Jaru at the hands of Leva. I saw my people that I had lived with become something that was nothing more than a mere shell of themselves, following Leva's orders and destroying her brother. They became the Ancients that only followed Leva, whom they called their queen, with no thoughts of their own."

"So how did you save Jaru then?" Calista frowned at him.

"We did!" The female Aggie stomped her foot. "Weren't you listening to me?" She pushed at Bastion who was watching her with adoration. He fell over but the smile never left his face.

"Careful Saint," Eryx cautioned. "You might hurt your new friend."

Bastion rolled over and rose to his feet, brushing the dust off. "Naw." He grinned at Saint. "She can push me over anytime she wants."

Saint gave a smile, then moved closer to Bastion who stood there grinning widely.

"Looks like you have a rival for Bastion's affections, Calista." Eon chuckled while his sister shot him a dirty look.

Saint frowned over at Calista who sighed. "Please ignore my little brother, Saint. Sometimes he knows not what he says." She shot him another dirty look when he opened his mouth. He shut it with a snap but the twinkle was there in his eyes. She gave another sigh and looked at Saint, hoping her brother hadn't upset the little Aggie. "How did you save him?"

"We brought his essence here and created this world for him to survive in, until Leva could be defeated and he could thrive again." Saint told them proudly.

Kaine frowned. "But you are all children of Ara, not Jaru. How is it that you're able to live here with Jaru?"

Grager stepped forward and spoke, "This world was created by us, not Jaru. He's visiting our world that we created to hide ourselves from Leva and her vengeance."

"Vengeance?" Calista frowned at the term that Grager used.

"We have much to discuss." Jaru moved forward and bowed slightly to the now disappearing Picknies. "I owe them much."

Calista turned to him and nodded. "Yes, we need your help in defeating the queen."

Jaru shook his head. "I can't defeat her."

"Is that why you're in hiding?" John asked him and Jaru nodded.

"Yes, in a way," he said.

"So, you're nothing more than a coward." Rikar growled at him.

He looked at Rikar. "No, I'm a realist. I'm unable to do any harm to my siblings."

"Even though she destroyed your world and children?" Eon asked.

Jaru nodded. "Even though she went against me, I still follow our father's rules."

Calista was curious about what he meant by their father's rules; especially since Gaia had said pretty much the same thing. But now wasn't the time for distractions. They had already strayed too far from their goal. She needed them back on track. She needed someone from here to help them devise a plan to defeat Leva. "Why?" Calista asked Jaru.

"Why what?" he asked her.

"Why hide? Your sisters believe you to be dead." Calista frowned. "I understand hiding from Leva, but your other sisters loved you, didn't they?"

"They did." He sighed, then shrugged. "I guess you can say I hid because what we did to our sister was wrong and we all deserved her anger." He sighed and looked at Eryx. "Though her people didn't, even though they took the blame so as not to blame the all-powerful Empyreans."

A short, stout male arrived, waddling side to side until he reached Jaru who grinned at him. "Let me introduce you to my mystic, Cleeve."

"I thought that Leva took your mystic as a prisoner and that he was used to help her destroy other worlds until she ran into the Criptines." Calista frowned when Jaru chuckled.

"I would tell you to be cautious about believing anything told to you by either of my sisters and their children." Jaru gave a wry smile. "Much of what they've said has been to hide what was done, unfortunately."

"So why should we believe you?" Rikar asked.

Jaru shrugged. "I have nothing, I'm in hiding, I have nothing to gain by lying."

"Except maybe your planet back," Calista suggested.

Jaru shook his head, a sad glint in his eyes. "No, once an Empyrean's world has been destroyed, it can't be rebuilt. The Primordial father had decreed that long ago. I have nothing to gain except to speak my own sins and hope that you lot are truly the ones to end this long sibling feud." He looked around at them all. "If you'll listen to me without constant interruptions. Then maybe, we can all find a suitable solution to this situation."

Calista turned to the others, finally facing everyone after the outburst between her and Rikar. "Maybe listening to what Jaru has to say will help us in stopping the queen. Maybe not." She shrugged. "But, what other option do we have? We need to stop her and after he tells his story, we can make our decision then."

"It could be just another waste of our time." Livinia used one of her blades to clean from under her fingernails while she spoke.

Calista nodded. "It could, or it could be the answers

we need. We won't know until we listen." When they still didn't look convinced, she tried a different tactic. "If we leave here now without listening, where will we go and what will we do? We need something more than we have."

Rikar moved forward, not as aggressively as before, but still guarded. "We'll listen, but make no other promises."

Calista nodded in agreement with him and turned to Jaru. "Let's hear your story."

Cleeve started moving things around a pit that appeared, one they hadn't seen before. This planet was as confusing as the inhabitants. Benches appeared from the ground and multi-colored fires erupted from the pit.

Jaru gestured to the pit and the benches. "Please sit and listen to my story." He watched them as each one moved to take a seat. Cleeve lumbered forward and took a seat on a small mound before the fire. Grager and Saint watched from the trees, while other Picknies faces appeared from their elements all around. Eryx took a seat on one of the outer benches and his son, Lantis, appeared next to his father.

Scratch rubbed against Calista's shoulder and pointed with one of his hairy legs to the sky. Butterflies with wings of birds flew around above them and raccoons with the beaks of birds watched them from the trees. This was truly a wondrous little world.

Jaru moved before them and stepped into the fire, his

voice echoing all around them. "I'm going to tell you a story of sibling love, rivalry, and even betrayal. Please listen carefully and maybe, just maybe ... you can right a wrong that was done long ago."

Chapter 20

The fire lit up and visions started playing, just as they had when Grint first told them the story of the Empyreans. They saw a void, nothing but darkness, in the flames as Jaru's disembodied voice started to speak.

"Life is born from darkness, though there has to be a creator."

A single light appeared in the void and started to grow. That light grew until it formed facial features. Eyes with black pupils, a nose that jutted with purpose, and firm lips on a commanding face.

"Meet the father of all creation, the Primordial. All creation came from him. He created the Empyreans; there are many of us but would allow only the direct familial link. He felt that too many siblings would create chaos, so he would create the siblings in sets of four. The Empyreans were one of the most powerful beings that the Primordial created, though they weren't the only ones."

The face stayed in the center while white lights would appear all around him, some showed almost translucent lines that would connect. Always in sets of four.

"Though, the Empyreans weren't the first ones created by the Primordial. Those would be called the Progenitors, or first born. They had no ties to any single celestial body, or any celestial being, except for the Primordial. They could travel throughout the stars into any area they wanted, they had no direct ties anywhere."

More lights appeared, though these had no lines connecting them to anything else.

"There were many other creations of the Primordial and they each had their own roles to play."

Other lights appeared; some smaller and some larger, some streaked across the darkness, and others soared with long lighted tails behind them.

"There were Protomarchs, Archons, Aeternals, Ascendants, and even Astral Regents. Many children of the Primordial had been created, and now they ruled the entire cosmos. The Primordial had given each of his children a set of rules that they were to follow, each cosmic hierarchy had a different set."

In the fire an image of Jaru and Gaia appeared, smiling out to them. They were joined by two more females. One female had ginger hair that flowed like lava while her skin shimmered as if made of colored water, the other female had beautiful crystal skin while her white hair flowed down her back almost to her feet.

"Must be Ara and Leva," Kaine said in a low tone to Calista. Though he attempted to be quiet, a wisp of flame still reached out to swat at him for daring to interrupt. She nodded in silent agreement, though she stayed silent to avoid her hand getting slapped.

"The Primordial gave the Empyreans a set of five rules they must follow, no exceptions," Jaru's voice continued from the fire.

"Rule number one was that no Empyrean may walk openly among their children. Our father believed that worship should be distant, that presence could corrupt evolution. This rule wasn't a hard one to follow for my siblings and myself. We enjoyed watching our children from afar, yet were able to distance ourselves."

Calista forgot about her vow to stay silent and spoke up, "but Gaia spoke to us in the grotto." She flinched when a flame moved towards her, though instead of slapping her hand, it wagged at her. Kaine grunted in annoyance but said nothing.

"Was this grotto out in the open where many others could see?" Jaru asked her. She gave a shake of her head. "Then she wasn't openly walking among her children."

"Technicalities," Calista grumbled, keeping her eye on the wisp of flame that gave a dismissive gesture before returning to the pit where Jaru continued.

"Rule number two was that no Empyrean may restore a world once it has fallen, nor could they interfere in the fall of another Empyrean. Our father gave us our one world, if we were unable to sustain it, then we weren't worthy of it. He was the father of all creation; he chose when new creations were to happen. He believed undoing loss would break the balance of cosmic order. When an Empyrean fell, he decreed there would be no rescues, no revenge, and above all else no wars between siblings."

Calista felt the urge to interrupt but she said nothing, decided to wait until he was finished to point out that Leva had surely not only tossed out that rule, but stomped on it. She looked around and from the tightened lips, she assumed they were all thinking the same thing.

"Rule number three was that Empyreans may guide, but never rule over their children, nor were they allowed to alter the nature of their children. He said his children were allowed to choose their own paths, so the children of his children should be given the same option. Gifts bestowed on their children for virtuous means were allowed, transformation, forbidden."

More glances were shared by Calista and the others upon hearing this, after all, that was another rule that Leva had broken and destroyed.

"The final rule our father handed down, and the one that he said was the most important. That breaking this rule would result in a punishment so severe, none of us wanted to think of it. He said that none of us may save our children from extinction."

"Not from war." Visions showed; battles on all of the Empyreans, even the one where Calista lost Solen. Seeing this vision had her throat constricting, while she attempted to swallow tears that started to form. She refused to let herself cry, not until they had completed Solen's mission. Then she could cry, break things, whatever made her feel better. Not now.

"Not from evolution." Visions showed them evolutions from each Empyrean. On Gaia you could see the ancient mortals evolving from earlier versions to the ones that now walk on Earth. The weather disasters that would take life and then the life that would grow from those disasters.

"Not from annihilation." The visions showed the battles of war again, and the dead bodies that littered the battlefield.

"Our children weren't meant to live forever; they were not strong enough to survive eternity. This rule was the hardest for all of us, to have children that followed us, and gave us such devotion. And we couldn't save them from death."

The vision showed all four together, the distaste on each of their faces over this rule was highly visible.

"We found ways around this, we gave our children the gift of prolonged life, though it had to come with conditions. They couldn't live forever, when the belief in them died, so would they. Though we could only give so many of these gifts, we had to be careful with our choosing. We cried that there were many other true and loyal children that deserved gifts as well."

In the vision they saw Aetherfall, with all the lands and people.

"Our father created Aetherfall for us, where our loyal children would be rewarded with an afterlife of comfort. It was a nice gift, but we still yearned to have contact with these children. We would sneak in, but this angered our father. He brought one of his Progenitors, Herman, to rule over Aetherfall, and to keep us from this realm."

Herman's face filled the vision, his expression was set, disciplined, and unmoved. But it wasn't his face that Calista took from what they just learned. "No parent should outlive their child," she said quietly.

Kaine looked at her with a frown. "Huh?"

She gave a small smile and explained, "just an Earth saying. No parent should outlive their child, it isn't natural." She gave a shrug. "Though it happens more than it should."

Jaru moved out of the fire to kneel down in front of Calista and looked at her, smiled at Scratch on her shoulder who watched him closely. "You understand that feeling, though your spider was brought back to life."

"Was that against the law?" Calista moved her hand to protectively hide Scratch, she feared for his life, she couldn't handle that again."

Jaru shook his head. "No, he hadn't died. Zeus preserved him before he died, and as Solen lay there dying, it was his right to give Scratch his remaining energy."

"What happens to the children that aren't loyal or

true to their Empyrean?" Allen asked. "Do they disappear into nothingness?"

Jaru stayed where he was, though his gaze did move from Calista to Allen. "They are reborn."

"And, if they still don't become true children?" Rikar asked him.

Jaru sighed. "They are reborn until they do, a never-ending cycle."

"Do they know that they've been reborn?" Cellica asked him. Sav watched from her seat, though she said nothing. Calista wondered if she already knew this, also wondered which part of the Primordial's children was she.

Jaru shook his head. "No, that would defeat the purpose of them becoming true children naturally. If they know they are being reborn, their loyalty might not be true."

Calista turned to Sav. "So, which of the children are you?"

Sav turned to her and for a moment, Calista wondered if she was going to answer, then with a shrug, Sav responded, "my tribe is part of the Aeternals. We exist where we choose, with any of our father's children. We are the advisors to the Primordial, though we mostly just observe, and report back to our father. He chooses whether to act or not. Sometimes, he sends us on missions, like the one I was sent on to locate Jaru."

"How couldn't he locate him?" Livinia asked. "He is

the Primordial, he should be able to locate anyone that he chooses."

Sav turned to her. "The Primordial hands down those laws for his children to follow, but he also has laws of his own. He doesn't interfere in the life of his children, unless they break a law. When that happens, he will be there, and he will hand down the punishment. Other than that, he relies on us, Aeternals, to report all to him."

Calista looked between Jaru and Sav, her brow furrowed in her confusion and wanting to understand all they were hearing. "Then where was he when Jaru was destroyed, Leva broke that law and many more. She walks among her subjects as queen, and it's very obvious that she has transformed her subjects into the parasites that they are. She even attempted to go after the Criptines, they had to defend themselves against her." Her head snapped back as a thought occurred to her. "Are the Criptines another Empyrean? Was that why they stopped helping Solen? Because they worried going against Leva would break one of the laws."

Jaru shook his head. "The Criptines were Progenitors, one of the first children of the Primordial. They answer to no one but our father. They were put into that position by Leva to interfere and so they joined with Solen to stop her. Due to what Leva had done, they were granted that right, but only for a certain time. They had their own duties that had to be attended to." Jaru gave

Calista a sympathetic look. "I'm sorry that they couldn't do more, but all of us have our own restrictions to abide by."

"Except that Leva had broken so many of your father's laws and yet remains unpunished." Calista crossed her arms with a frown. "How is it that she is still allowed to run around unhindered? I know Gaia said that she was cut off from your father, but still, that doesn't seem like a punishment deserving of all of her crimes. I mean, she kills a brother, and her father cuts her off? Whoopee." Calista sneered.

Jaru snorted. "Gaia told you that she was cut off from our father after my slightly exaggerated demise?"

Calista frowned. "You're saying that she wasn't cut off from your father?"

"Not at all." He shook his head. "She was, but long before that, and without proof of my demise, my father wouldn't hand down a punishment for that. And as you can see, I'm alive and well."

"Wouldn't Gaia and Ara know that?" Kaine asked.

Jaru nodded. "They would, but they feel safer if they bury their heads in the sand, and pretend otherwise. They don't want their children to know what they had done, what we had done to our sister long ago."

"What do you mean?" Calista frowned.

CHAPTER 21

Jaru turned back to the pit, where the fire still roared with visions. "I told you of my father's laws that he handed down as absolute," he said quietly. "There was one law the four of us could never accept. The final law. The one my father valued above all others."

He looked up into the sky, possibly to where his world once stood. "We were forbidden to interfere. Forbidden to save them." His voice tightened. "Our children were dying, entire lineages fading into nothing, and we were made to watch. Even those children we cherished above all others were not spared."

He turned to Calista. "You said no parent should outlive their child. Yet we did, again and again. Each time a child passed into Aetherfall, knowing we would never hear their voice again, something was taken from us. Something that never returned."

When he turned back to the fire, there were visions of all the siblings standing together.

"We all agreed the fourth law was cruel. Unnecessary. A demand too far. We wanted to confront our father, but we feared him. Even then." A hollow breath escaped him. "Gaia suggested we stand together; four voices as one. Surely, he couldn't dismiss us all."

The flames dimmed slightly.

"Ara argued that too many voices might sound like chaos. That one of us should speak, carrying the will of the others." Jaru's gaze dropped. "It was my idea that Leva should be that voice."

Pain crept into his tone, slow and unmistakable.

"She was the most level-headed among us. The most patient. And she held more of our father's favor than any of us. I believed, truly believed, that if anyone could make him listen, it would be her."

The fire showed it then.

Leva stood before the Primordial's vast presence, radiant and unflinching. The other three; Gaia, Ara, and Jaru, remained behind her.

"She spoke calmly," Jaru continued. "She told him we would honor every other law. That we would obey him in all things; except this one. Our children were too precious. Too irreplaceable."

The fire darkened. The Primordial's eyes narrowed.

"Even as his anger filled the space around us, Leva did not waver. She did not beg. She did not soften her words." Jaru swallowed. "She spoke as a daughter who still believed she could be heard."

Then the Primordial spoke.

The fire surged, the face within it growing vast,

overwhelming. The voice thundered around them, ancient and absolute.

"You stand before me and call my law unjust? Before me, your father and creator?"

The flames twisted violently with each word that was spoken. Sparks flew as if the fire felt the anger of the Primordial.

"I gave you existence. I gave you purpose. I asked for obedience, and in return, I gave you order. I gave you meaning."

The face turned to the others who stood there staring at their father in fear of his anger. Calista shook her head; she had a bad feeling she knew where this was going.

"And you? Do you stand with your sister?"

The trio stood there in silence for a moment, a brief moment as their father waited for their answer. Then, one by one, each hammered the nails into Leva's coffin. Gaia lowered her eyes. Ara turned away. And Jaru, he shook his head. Leva turned to them, disbelief written across her face. No fear, no anger there, only the look of total betrayal.

"They promised her," Jaru said, his voice barely above a whisper. "We all did." The weight of guilt that could be heard in his voice, weighed down on all those who sat in disbelief of what they were hearing.

The sound of sparks flying from the fire, pulled their attention back to the visions in the flame. The Primordial turned from the trio, and now he stared at Leva, who stared at her siblings with such pain that Calista felt for her. Even knowing all that she'd done. The primordial then spoke, with each word the fire twisted and roared, Leva turned to look at her father.

"You call defiance love," he said. "You call rebellion mercy. Very well."

Gone was the trio from the vision. Gone was the face of the Primordial. Only the face of Leva as she listened to her father hand down a punishment that should've been shared between the siblings, but instead, landed completely on her.

"For your betrayal of my law, your bond to me shall be severed. For your refusal to yield, your bond to your siblings shall be broken," Leva cried out at his words, not in pain, but in shock at the depth of punishment. "Until you repent," the Primordial continued, unmoved. "You will feel no connection, no unity, no comfort in the family unit. You will learn why my laws exist, and why they are absolute."

The vision shattered and the fire that once roared was gone as if it had never been there. Jaru stared into the empty pit. His words were spoken so softly, that they had to strain to hear him. "My father believed he was preserving creation," he said. "And Leva... he believed she was the one who betrayed him." They watched as a single tear rolled down his cheek, something that shocked Calista, she didn't think an Empyrean could cry.

"So, you see, my sisters and I are at fault for any

atrocities that Leva has created," he ended on a somber note. "We attempted to apologize to Leva after that, but she refused to see any of us, and said we were no longer connected. She said we were no longer siblings."

"Can you blame her?" Livinia looked at him, her gaze hard and unforgiving. "Because of your cowardice she was damned."

Jaru nodded. "I know."

"Did any of you think that if you had stood with her, maybe he would've relented like Gaia suggested?" Rikar stared at Jaru, too stunned by what he had learned to show any anger.

Another nod. "Yes, many times. But it was too late. We tried to explain it to ourselves and justify our reactions. Better for one to take the fall than all three, after all, we had our children to think of."

"That is called justification, and holds no real truth," Calista countered and he nodded in agreement.

"So, you decided to hide the truth of what you've done, and let your sister bear the brunt of all the blame?" Kaine asked, though it was more of a statement. He gave a look of disgust at Jaru's nod. "So, all my years worshipping Ara were lies?"

Jaru looked at him. "No, not lies. We love our children. We wanted to fight for our children."

"You didn't though." Calista rose and stared at him. "Leva did and she paid the price. Not sure if I truly want to save any of you, you deserve her anger."

Jaru nodded. "You're right, we do, but our children don't. To destroy us, she needs to destroy our children as well. I listened to the cries of my children as Leva tore through them, destroyed them one by one before she finally started tearing me apart. I'm not asking you to save us, I'm asking you to save our children, which most here are."

Calista walked away from him in agitation, she hated this. He was right, and yet he was wrong. It felt as if they were once again hiding from accountability. They shouldn't be able to get away with what they had done.

She stared around her at the beauty she saw, the tiny eyes of the Picknies that watched her, as if her decision decided their lives. It probably did; something else that didn't sit well with her. She turned to look at Jaru, her mind made up. "We'll help stop your sister, save the innocents that don't deserve her wrath." When Jaru opened his mouth, possibly to thank her, she didn't know. She raised her hand to hold him off. "On one condition."

She smiled when his eyes narrowed at her. "Condition?" he asked.

She nodded, and he motioned for her to continue. "We stop her, and then you admit to your father what you and your sisters did. I won't attempt to stop her, unless the three of you finally take accountability."

He frowned at her. "You don't think I've taken accountability? I've lost my children. I'm hiding out on a small meteorite rather than ruling a world." She raised a brow in disbelief. "I've faced my consequences."

She snorted. "Not with your father, you haven't." She stared at him, unmoving and resolute in her decision. When the others moved from their seats to stand behind her, she smiled and when she felt Rikar's hand on her shoulder, her smile widened even more. "This is what family does. Even when you're mad at one another, you still have their back." Rikar's hand gave a gentle squeeze that she understood was his agreement.

She took a moment to swallow the emotion that rose within her, then she turned her attention back to Jaru. "What's your decision?"

He looked around and finally nodded. "I guess I don't have a choice, I agree." He gave a sigh. "It's time for the truth to come out."

"How do we know you'll keep your word?" Rikar asked. "After all, you betrayed your own sister. None of us here are your children."

Calista stared at Jaru, Rikar had a great point. But it wasn't Jaru that answered, Sav moved forward. "He'll keep his word. If I have to bring him to our father and make him admit it myself," she spoke, her gaze hard.

"Well, then," Calista looked to Sav then back to Jaru. "It's time to finish this. How do we stop your sister?"

Eryx moved forward. "You must find the heart of Leva."

"What do you mean?" Kaine asked, his confusion mirrored on all their faces.

"All Empyreans have a heart," Eryx told them.

"Well, yeah," Calista said slowly. "Are you saying that we have to cut out her heart?" They each had a look of disgust on their face. They wanted to defeat her, but not dissect her.

Eryx chuckled. "No, you won't be cutting out her heart. Every mystic is charged with caring for the heart of their empyrean." Eryx gave a wave of his hand.

Cleeves lumbered forward and looked up at Jaru, who nodded in agreement. "Do it, Cleeves." With a shrug Cleeves held out his stubby hand that was clenched into a loose fist. As they watched, a staff appeared in his grip, at the end was a blue jewel that sparkled. "Our hearts aren't like yours; they are our gifts to our mystics. They give our mystics certain powers to do our biddings."

The fire behind them lit up and there they saw four staffs, each with a colored gem. "The blue gem is mine," Jaru told them, as he spoke the staffs moved until the blue one was front and center. "The green one is Gaia's." The green moved to the front. "The white one is Ara's." The white one moved. "And the one you need to find is the red one that belongs to Leva." The staff with the bright red gem moved until it was in front.

Calista turned to Eryx and held out her hand. "So, give us the heart and tell us what we need to do with it, so we can finish this."

He grimaced. "I wish it was that easy."

Calista let out a harsh breath and fixed him with a tired stare. "Easy?" She echoed. "Nothing about this has been easy. We hunted the Ancients, tore down their prisons, chased rumors of a queen who never appeared. Then we finally go home; only to be dragged before Gaia and put through her trials, as if we haven't suffered enough."

Her hands clenched at her side. "We find a mystic who isn't there. We're sent halfway across existence to learn how to destroy Leva. And now you tell us you wish it were simple?" Her voice sharpened. "Then stop dancing around it. Tell us what has to be done. Let us finish this, so we can go back to whatever pieces of our lives that still remain."

Eryx raised a brow and nodded. "Very well then, I've hidden the heart, in case Leva were to capture me."

"And where did you hide it?" Rikar asked, folding his arms.

He grinned. "I've hidden it on a moon of Ara, the farthest from the planet. One where no life is thriving, the world is cold and unforgiving. Look for a cave where no light can shine, although red flowers thrive within. Among those flowers, you'll find the heart."

Calista looked over at Kaine and Allen. "Do you know the moon that he is talking about?"

Kaine nodded. "Yeah, but he isn't kidding about it being unforgiving. We'll need to get the heart and leave as quickly as possible."

Calista nodded, that was her plan anyways. She turned back to Eryx and Jaru. "What do we do after we find the heart? How do we stop the queen?"

"That will be tricky, there are many things to take into consideration," Jaru told her. "Our hearts are not meant to be kept within; they stay with our mystics so that we have a connection with them. Leva has had no connection with Eryx, nor her heart in so long. Our hope is that if you're able to put her heart back within her body, that maybe, just maybe it will start to heal her damaged soul."

"How do I put the heart back within her?" Calista frowned. "Stab her in the chest with it?" She shrugged, having no idea other than that.

Jaru shook his head. "No, nothing as barbaric as that. All you need to do is let the heart touch her chest, though if she sees what you're doing, she'll be able to harden herself against the heart. You'll need her distracted, so that she won't realize what you're attempting to do."

"I need to touch the heart to her chest without her realizing I'm doing it?" Calista stared at him incredulously. "Exactly, how am I going to do that?"

Jaru handed her a vial of shiny dust, one that resembled the ones of Ara and Gaia she had back on the ship.

"You're essence?" she asked him. When he nodded, she frowned at him. "I thought they were supposed to lead me to her; how will they help me force her to hold her heart for a full minute?"

"After you find her heart, take these three vials and place them on your navigation console. Do not open them, under any circumstance, do not open them." He stared at her, not saying anything, as if he needed her acceptance before he continued. When she nodded in agreement, he continued. "The ship will fly you to her, just as it flew you here. When you land, put these vials someplace safe. Somewhere she can't see them, that is very important, Leva can't see them."

"Why?" Calista frowned but Jaru just shook his head.

"Trust me on this, they must stay sealed, and hidden until the moment you need them," he told her.

"And when will that be?" She frowned at him.

"When you have her weakened enough that you think you have a chance of placing her heart on her chest, that is when you'll take these three vials, uncork them, and then pour them into the ground at her feet. All three must be poured at the same time," he told her with the same urgency. "Remember that, it's very important."

"Then what?" Calista looked down at the vial and then back up at Jaru.

"Then, you'll place the heart on her breast," Jaru told her. "Let her heart reunite with her soul, let her feel all the pain that she has caused, and pray with me that it isn't too late for her."

"What does that mean?" Calista frowned at him, but he just gave a sad smile and disappeared from sight. She looked around and saw that Eryx, Lantis, Cleeves, and most of the Picknies were gone as well. Only her crew stood there now, well, them and Saint. Calista frowned when she saw another female Aggie standing next to Saint. "Who're you?" she asked.

The Aggie tossed her rainbow hair with hues of red at the end, something she was sure no other Aggie had, and spoke with confidence. "My name is Trish and wherever Saint goes, I go as well." Her arms crossed, as she dared any of them to contradict her.

Calista looked at Bastion who gave a bashful smile. "We have new crew members," he said with a big smile.

Calista sighed. "Let's go and get this over with. Time to head to Ara."

CHAPTER 22

Calista leaned back in her favorite seat in the dining room, a hot steaming mug of Jazzy juice in her hand. They were on their way to Ara's moon. The crew were making good use of their down time, whether it be to prepare for the upcoming battle, or to rest up for it.

Saint and Trish had made themselves right at home in Bastion's Arboretum, not that Bastion was complaining. He enjoyed having more Aggies on the ship and he must've told them about Allen's attempt at dinner. Anytime he neared the Arboretum, the girls would give him side-eyes and watch him carefully. Thankfully, he never attempted to enter. Calista didn't want to think what those two would do.

So far, since joining the crew, she's had to deal with complaints about the girls and their hijinks. Stryx used the voice comm only to have his voice sound like a squeaky toy, Bastion apologized profusely and promised to fix it. No one knew what Stryx had done to get on the girl's bad side, but he kept his distance from them after that.

They had even messed with Cellica's music in her

room, though Cellica just danced to it anyways. She said it was much faster than what she was used to, but she enjoyed the challenge. John had become Cellica's constant companion now, he watched over her and would make sure she had anything she needed or desired.

Other than the two troublemakers and the two lovebirds, the voyage had been uneventful. Something Calista was thankful for. That peace shattered the moment the door to her dining room slid open and Rikar stepped inside. So much for uneventful.

She set her mug aside and watched as he chose a lounge across from her, sitting stiffly, as if unsure whether he should be there at all. Silence stretched between them.

"Hi," he said at last.

"Hi," she replied, the word feeling inadequate the moment it left her mouth.

Rikar stared at the floor for a long moment before he looked back up at her. "I want to apologize," he said, then stopped. A breath left him, rough and uneven. "But I can't. Not honestly."

Calista's chest tightened.

"I know you didn't cause what happened to Draken," he continued. "I know that. I've told myself that more times than I can count." His jaw clenched. "This isn't about blame."

"Then what is it about?" she asked him, her tongue darting out to moisten her dry lips. Honestly, she didn't know where they went wrong either. When they no longer could talk or laugh together.

In his eyes she saw so many raw emotions of pain, anger, and something she couldn't define. "It's that I followed you," he said. "That we both followed you and he didn't return. We didn't have to, I know that. No one forced us to follow you."

He stood up and started pacing the room, so much emotion radiated off of him, that it almost choked her. "Every part of me understands the truth, but understanding doesn't stop the anger." He turned to stare at her with a pained look. "And it doesn't bring him back."

Calista swallowed hard, she felt as if she had a baseball sized lump in her throat. She stayed silent, she didn't even know if she had a voice to respond.

"I love you," Rikar told her. "You're family. That hasn't changed, no matter what has been said." His voice lowered. "But forgiveness..." He shook his head. "I don't know if I have that in me, maybe I never will."

He didn't wait for her answer. The door slid shut behind him, leaving Calista alone. She sat there staring at the empty lounge seat across from her. She wasn't sure whether she'd just lost something, or if it had been gone all along.

A single tear rolled down her cheek, the only emotion that she allowed herself.

"Calista! Rikar! Kaine!" Stryx's voice came over

the com system, thankfully no squeaks could be heard. "Show time, guys!"

They rushed to the bridge, where the vision of the moon showed brightly. They stared at the image on the view screen. The moon resembled a ball of ice. Calista shivered looking at it.

"I would suggest all of you bundle up." Stryx moved from the pilot's chair to a nearby wall where he pushed a button. The wall opened to reveal cold-weather clothing and necessities of all sizes.

Kaine looked at him. "Not joining us?"

Stryx snorted. "No thanks, I'll stay here where it's nice and warm. Privileges of being a captain." He grinned.

"Outta the way." Trish pushed past them into the closet and started pulling on a tiny snow outfit, boots and all. Saint followed her, pulling Bastion along as well.

Livinia looked down at them with a frown. "What do you guys think you're doing?"

"We're going with," Saint told them as she dressed.

"Don't try to stop us," Trish warned as she moved out of the closet, already fully dressed for the winter moon.

"We might have family there," Bastion attempted to explain, though it was hard when the girls were pulling him along with them.

Livinia looked at Calista who just shrugged as she moved into the closet and started pulling on her warm outfit. "I'm not arguing with them, if you want to, go for it."

"Great, going to be overrun by little people before too long," Kaine muttered. The room went silent and Calista groaned, looking out towards the bridge where Trish and Saint paused in pulling Bastion. They both turned to look at Kaine, their eyes narrowed on him for a few moments, before they turned back around and kept pulling Bastion along. Kaine cursed while the others chuckled.

"Too bad, man," Rikar gripped his shoulder as he moved past, all suited up. "I'll make sure to give your eulogy at your funeral." Kaine shot him a baleful look.

Calista sighed while her and Livinia stood outside the closet, pulling on the remainder of their outfit. Livinia frowned at Calista. "How will we find this cave and the heart?"

Before Calista could admit that she didn't know and wondered the same thing, Sav spoke up, "I'm able to sense the Empyreans, which would also mean their hearts."

Calista pursed her lips together for a moment. "Guess you get to go play in the snow with the rest of us." She looked at everyone. "Let's go find the heart and finish this."

The wind whipped around them as they walked through the snow, they pulled their hoods closer around their face while they kept moving. They followed Sav who kept moving with purpose. When they first landed, Sav said she couldn't feel anything, so they walked for several hours before Sav revealed that she could finally feel the heart. That was over an hour ago.

Stryx told them they couldn't be down here longer than five hours, and they were coming up on that limit quickly.

"If she doesn't find the heart soon, we'll have to head back to the ship," Livinia shouted, the wind whipping her words from her mouth.

Calista nodded in agreement. Even as a goddess, this weather was unforgiving and cruel. Just as she was about to announce it was time to head back, there was a light ahead. She looked over at Sav, who had stopped and was now staring at that same light. "Is that the heart?" She shouted, the wind starting to gain in momentum. Sav gave a shake of her head.

A shout could be heard in the air and when they looked, they saw Trish being flung around by the wind, Saint attempted to grab her but she was thrown back by another gust of wind. If not for Kaine, Trish would've been flying on the wind. Rikar reached down and grabbed Saint before she could be thrown airborne as well.

"Help!" Bastion shouted as he was tossed into the air by another stray gust of wind. Livinia attempted to grab him by one of her braids but the wind changed direction and pulled him away from her braids.

"Bastion!" Both Saint and Trish called out, but he kept rising higher. Calista attempted to shimmer him to her but she couldn't get a hold on him with the wind jerking him around. She was about to launch herself into the air to grab him, when he jerked in the air and was pulled down towards the light ahead of them.

Calista looked over at Sav and the others for just a moment before she took off towards the light, towards their little friend. Knowing they should be heading back to the ship, but no way would they leave Bastion. The light was their only guide as they ran through the snow.

The light seemed to grow as they got closer, until they saw the opening of a cave. They got closer and realized that there was a fire burning in the cave, even closer and they saw Bastion huddled around the fire, all alone. They entered the cave cautiously, looking around but seeing no one but Bastion. Saint and Trish jumped down and ran to Bastion, hugging him close, before they backed away and slapped him, to the amazement of the others.

"That's for scaring us like that." Saint told him, then they each sat on the other side of him to enjoy the fire.

"Bastion?" Calista moved closer to the fire.

"Yes?" Bastion looked up at her.

"How did you get in here?" she asked him, then she looked at the fire. "How did this get here?"

Bastion grinned and pointed to the mouth of the cave. They turned around to see a bunch of smaller figures move into the cave. When the light hit them, Calista gasped, "Those are the Jinsons." She turned back to Bastion who grinned and nodded. She turned back to them. "How did you guys get here?" she asked them.

The Jinsons moved forward, their skin a sparkling blue, while the fur that covered their hands and feet were different colors. They had neutral earthtones, bright colors of every kind, and even some were a multitude of colors. The claws on the feminine looking Jinsons looked as if they had been colored, while the ones on the more masculine ones looked to be either clear or dark, but no colors.

One of them moved forward, his ice blue skin looked hard rugged, as if made of diamonds. His fur was of darkened earthtones while his nails were longer, darker, and sharper than the others. "My name is Chaffer." His voice was gruff and he spoke slowly, pronouncing each word carefully as he watched them. "I am the chief of the Jinsons."

Bastion grinned up at Calista. "They made their homes here after the great war," he told her with a grin. She was thankful that Bastion took over the explanation, she wasn't sure they had the time to wait for Chaffer to tell them that. "Jinsons thrive in this weather."

"How did they know that they would be able to live on this moon?" Kaine asked Bastion, though it was Chaffer that answered.

"All of us Picknies have that knowledge," he told

him, his piercing blue eyes looking right at Kaine. "Ara's moons were created for the Picknies, a place to go if ever needed, and still be close to Ara."

Bastion frowned at him. "I didn't know that," he protested.

A smaller, feminine Jinson moved closer, her fur a nice emerald color while her nails were a bright pink. "That knowledge was kept with the chief of the clan." Her voice was higher pitched, though not as slow as Chaffer's. Then her eyes looked down and her voice lowered slightly. "With the death of Sanders, the Aggies lost that knowledge." She gave a small smile. "Though now, you can tell the others."

"Brit!" Chaffer frowned at her.

"But he can, papa!" Brit protested.

"I would rather be back on Ara," Bastion said lowly. The girls and the Jinsons all lowered their heads and nodded.

Brit looked over at him, her eyes narrowing as if a thought suddenly occurred to her. "If you didn't know of the moons, why are you here?"

"We're here for the heart of Leva," Calista told them. "The heart of the queen. We need it to finish this, to stop her from harming anyone else."

Brit frowned at her. "What does it look like?"

"Like the heart of Ara, except different. Red in color, rather than white," Bastion told them.

Brit bit her lip, then turned swiftly and ran towards

the back of the cave. Calista frowned and looked at the others, who wore the same confused expression.

"Brit is young and impulsive," Chaffer explained in his slow way. He waved a weathered hand, his nails glinting in the light. "What will you do when you locate the heart? Will you be able to heal Ara?" he asked. "We have many refugees from Ara who want to return home, some have even taken refuge on the other moons."

Calista sighed and gave a sad smile. "I don't know if we will be able to heal Ara, but we'll stop the queen from harming anyone else."

"Here it is!" Brit ran up to them, holding the staff with the red jewel proudly in her claws. "We found it many years ago among some red flowers, when placed beneath the light, it would brighten up our room."

"Thank you." Calista smiled and reached for the heart. She frowned when Brit pulled it back. "What?"

"After you defeat the queen, will you promise to find the refugees of Ara?" Brit asked her. "Bring the ones that want to live on the moons here?"

Calista nodded. "We will, and we'll also offer them a place on Gaia, in our home if they so choose."

Brit smiled at her and handed her the heart. "Good luck, child of Ara."

Chapter 23

They had placed all three unopened vials of the essences on the navigation panel, where they started to glow softly and then just like before, the ship was on auto pilot. This time, they knew where they were going, they were heading for the queen.

The final fight.

Calista stood in the dining room, a steaming mug of Jazzy juice in her hand, and her gaze on the stars passing by the ship. She closed her eyes when she heard the door silently open. She sent a silent prayer that it was anybody but Rikar. She didn't think she could handle another of their heart to hearts, not when she was doing her best to psych herself up before the upcoming fight.

"Sis."

She turned at Eon's voice and smiled at her brother. "Eon." They barely had any time together since they started on this mission, a part of her had wondered if her brother had been avoiding her. When he didn't move, she frowned at him. "Are you okay?"

He moved closer to her and pulled her into a hug, his arms wrapped around her, and squeezed gently.

She wrapped her arms around him and laid her head on his chest, holding him close. A smile tugging at her lips, the last time they had hugged, he had been so much smaller. Now, he towered over her, his cheek lay on the top of her head.

She pulled back and looked up at him. "Tell me what's wrong, Eon," she told him, her hand cupping his cheek.

He sighed and pressed his cheek against her hand, looking into her eyes. "Promise me that you're coming home with us."

She frowned. "I can't make that promise, I wish I could. I know I can't go home until the queen has been defeated."

"And once she's been defeated?" he asked her.

"Eon, what are you trying to say?" Calista felt Scratch stirring on her shoulder, peering out to see Eon there, then moving back to rest beneath her hair.

"I don't want you to do something stupid," he said as he stepped away from her, looking anywhere but at her. "I know you miss Solen, and I know you would do anything to be with him –"

"Stop," Calista interrupted him, turning him back to face her. "I won't do anything stupid, I promise," she told him.

"Are you sure?" he asked her.

She sighed and looked out into space. She hadn't told anyone, but her mother, about what happened when she became the fire of Ara, she couldn't stand to repeat it. But this was her brother, and she needed to reassure him. She looked back at him, her eyes watery as she remembered. "When I became the fire of Ara, I spoke with Solen." Her throat constricted when she said his name.

Eon frowned. "You did?" She gave a shaky nod. "You never told any of us this."

She gave a shrug. "I couldn't," she said, her voice hoarse. "Every time I think of it, I get choked up." She gave a watery smile, then breathed in deep, before she continued. "But I promised him that I would live for him, so you see, I can't do anything stupid," she said and a single tear escaped, rolling down her cheek.

Eon moved and pulled her into his arms. "I'm sorry, sis. I didn't mean to make you cry, I just worried about you."

She wrapped her arms around him and shook her head against his chest. "It's okay." She sighed, and after several moments she pulled away and smiled at him. "We'll be okay, and go home soon."

They sat there in the dining room, staring out at the stars for several hours before her brother spoke again. "Doesn't any of this seem odd to you?" he asked her.

"Any of what?" She looked over at him.

"The fact that since we left Earth and headed to Jaru, that we haven't come across any Ancients. For years, they hunted us, even as we hunted them." He frowned. "Now, suddenly, we've had months with no contact." He shrugged. "It just doesn't feel right."

"I don't know," she admitted. "All we can do is hope that they are running scared."

"Sometimes that can be worse." Eon grimaced.

"Everyone, front and center." Stryx's voice came loud and clear over the voice coms.

They looked at each other, and took deep breaths, rose, and then headed towards the bridge. They ran into Kaine, Allen, and Sav in the hallway. Together they moved to the bridge, almost tripping over Bastion, Saint, and Trish who ran beneath their legs to run past them. They arrived to see Rikar, Livinia, John, and Cellica already there.

Calista looked at Stryx. "We there?" she asked him.

He nodded and handed her the three vials that no longer glowed. "We're here, and we have problems."

"What?" She frowned, when he nodded towards the view screen, she turned and her stomach dropped.

"Well, we wondered where the Ancients were." Her brother grimaced.

There, in front of them were over a dozen Ancient ships. They could see their home world, or what was left of it, behind them. That must be where the queen was, they were protecting their queen. "She must've called them all home." Calista stared, those were some pretty big ships.

"Any way that you can summon that power you used on Ara?" Rikar asked her.

Calista slowly shook her head. "I don't even know

how I did it, not to that magnitude. I might be able to do some damage to the ships but not enough to obliterate them like I did before."

"So, how do we get past them?" Kaine asked, glaring at the ships.

"I would say, you need a distraction." Stryx breathed in deeply.

Rikar stared at him. "That's not a distraction; that's a suicide run."

"Call it what you want, but it's your only way to the queen." Stryx breathed deeply and shrugged. "Everyone on this trip knew there was a chance they weren't coming home."

"Not by suicide." Rikar growled, while Calista shook her head.

"There must be another way," Calista implored him.

Stryx chuckled. "This won't be a suicide run; you think those silver-tongued robots are any match for my ship?" He grinned at Cellica and gave her a wink, ignoring the frown on John's face. "There is more to this ship than what you can see."

"Stryx!" Calista protested but he held up a hand and looked at her with that burning expression of his.

"Did you come here to defeat the queen or argue?" he asked her. When no one said anything, he gave a curt nod. "Okay, get geared up, those who can move without a ship will escort those who need to use the shuttle craft. We'll distract the ships while you all get to the planet and defeat the queen." When Livinia opened her mouth, he gave a shake of his head. "Not another word, just go."

Calista swallowed hard and then nodded as they left the bridge. Her, Rikar, and Eon prepared themselves for their flight through space. When Sav joined them, rather than get into the shuttle with the others, Calista raised her brows. "Aeternals don't need ships?"

Sav gave a shake of her head, but said nothing as she stood there with them before the bay doors. Stryx's voice echoed from the voice com. "When the fighting starts, Vestor will open the bay doors. We'll hold their attention long enough for you to land. Good luck, everyone, we'll see one another again."

Calista swallowed her protest before it could become words. The war had stripped too much from them already. The crew, once strangers, were family now, and they were about to throw themselves against the full force of the Ancient fleet. She inhaled deeply, steadying herself. If she lost focus now, they wouldn't make it through the battle, let alone down to the planet.

The queen had a lot to answer for.

The sound of war raged outside as the bay doors opened. Calista drew in a steady breath, letting her energy flow around her just as the air was ripped away, following the shuttle into the void. A phoenix encased Calista as she lifted herself up and left the ship, Rikar in full dragon flew along next to her. Eon encased himself in his time orb where the rings of time rotated around him. Sav became a being of complete light and joined them.

They moved through space as Stryx fired on the ships, keeping their attention just as he said he would. The vessel transformed mid-battle, metal folding and roaring into the shape of a colossal dragon. Energy blazed from its jaws, tearing through the Ancients, while its tail snapped outward, gouging a deep trench through an enemy ship.

The ship looked magnificent, and gave Calista hope that they could win this battle. The Ancients converged on the mighty metal dragon until they could see nothing but the lights of the battle. She turned away and followed the shuttle to the planet, or what was left of it. Scratch clung to her neck, safely ensconced in the little bubble she created for him.

Calista's feet touched the ground, staring around her at what was left of Leva's world. Leva had done a lot of wrong to a lot of people, and while she was wronged, it didn't excuse all the lives she destroyed. Kaine, John, Allen, Cellica, Bastion, Trish, and Saint exited the shuttle looking bemused at all that they saw.

Calista couldn't blame them, after all, there was hardly anything left of this world but yet there was an atmosphere and a gravity that kept them from flying into space. This world reminded her of the post-apocalyptic movies that the mortals always enjoyed watching. They all walked down a path that wove between barren lands and ruined buildings. Dead trees and bones littered the landscape.

They continued walking, Sav in the lead, looking like the girl they first met. She stopped when they came to a building that stood several stories high. The only building that didn't look as if it had been ravaged by time, war, or both. Wooden arches, crystal walls and shiny metal statues all around the building. Wooden roots and vines wove all around, hanging from doorways and windows. The main doorway stood wide open, as if inviting them in for dinner.

Before they could enter, several Ancients appeared, not from the temple but around it. They said nothing though they continued to move towards them, their empty eyes watching their movements. They moved in front of the building, blocking them from entering.

"We need to move them but we can't let them touch us." Calista looked around them and sighed.

Kaine moved forward, his hands glowing brightly. "I have an idea." He turned to Allen. "Did you bring your bow and arrows?"

Allen snorted. "Of course." He pulled out his bow and arrows, frowning when Kaine grabbed two of his arrows.

"Think you can do that double shot your brother used to do?" he asked Allen, who frowned but nodded.

Then Kaine held onto the two arrows and they started to glow brightly. Kaine pointed to the vines that hung from the large doorway. "Can you hit those with them?"

Allen took both arrows with an eyeroll. "Can an Aggie jump through trees?" He cocked the arrow and let them fly. They hit the vines and exploded, raining sparks around the doorway, and sending the Ancients scattering.

"Let's go!" Kaine shouted.

They all ran past the recovering Ancients, through the doorway, where they turned to face the Ancients. They expected the Ancients to follow them in, but they stood there, as if they couldn't enter.

"Do you think the queen is refusing them entry?" Allen asked, frowning.

"Don't know, don't care." Calista sighed. "Just thankful. Let's see if we can find her." She turned and started down the long hallway, unsure of what was ahead.

Chapter 24

So, you think you're able to defeat me."

The feminine voice echoed all around them, bouncing off the dry dirt walls, as they moved deeper into the temple. Though, looking around, they would have thought they were moving deeper into the planet itself, which was a good possibility.

"Such pitiful little creatures, with their little gifts. Gifts that won't help them in this battle."

The voice of the Empyrean echoed through the planet's dead veins, feminine and commanding. Her words undercut by a jagged, unhinged laughter that rolled along the barren walls, as though the dying world itself had lost its mind.

Calista felt a trickle of fear roll down her spine, not fear for herself, but for all those that she cared about. Stryx and the crew that fought in the space above them, a fight where they were grossly outnumbered.

Rikar, who walked alongside her, and who has always been more of a brother than anything to her. Their disagreements meant nothing right now.

The pain.

The anger.

All stupid emotions considering what they were walking into.

Her brother who walked tall and proud on the other side, glowing time rings circling his clenched hands. He had seen so much heartache already, his words back on the ship revealed his fear that rode him now. But yet, he walked alongside her with no hesitation.

Kaine.

Livinia.

John.

Cellica.

Sav.

They walked into the battle together, even the three little Aggies who moved with careful steps. Whether they had stayed on the ship or entered the eerie cavern, the danger would've been the same. Their lives were already at risk, so they chose to fight.

She took a deep breath and paused in her stride, the others followed suit and watched her with faces full of questions, though none said a thing. She didn't know if this would work, but she was done walking through these earthen caverns with a voice echoing around them. A voice that could strike anytime without warning.

Time to bring the queen to them. With a touch, she sent Scratch from her shoulder to hide in a rut in the wall. She moved forward, motioning for the others to stay back. "Leva!" She shouted.

The cavern stayed silent.

"I know that you were wronged," she shouted out, ignoring the frowns from the others. "That your siblings didn't stand with you, like they had promised they would."

"Wronged?" The wind whipped around them so hard that they had to bring up their arms to block the sand, twigs, and rocks that were flung with that one word. Before them, they saw a set of dark eyes full of anger. "I was betrayed!"

More wind picked up around them, the Aggies shrieked as they were tossed into the air. If not for Livinia and her braids, they would've been thrown against the walls.

The walls around them began to shift, dirt shifting away as skeletons eased forward. Their bones twisting and unfolding from their compacted graves until they dragged themselves upright once more. A film of skin began to crawl over their bare frames; muted and ashen. Lacking the Ancient's silver glow, closer to those they had met in Aetherfall, but faded and imperfect.

"I'll leave you to play with your cousins, while I take care of those pesky traitors in the sky." Leva's deranged laugh followed her words. "Have fun, children."

Calista looked around them, attempting to calculate how many dead were appearing, but each time she thought she had a number, more appeared.

"I hate zombie shows." Eon groaned, a feeling she

shared. She never watched them on Earth, and had no desire to be in the middle of one. The closest she came to enjoying anything zombie, was that one comic book that Eon had bought at a con many years back.

Rikar growled. "Time to send these guys back to their graves!" With a roar he transformed into his big blue dragon, spewing his blue fire at the zombies. Their skin would melt off, but yet their bones still walked towards them, while more skin would crawl back onto the bone. With a swipe of his mighty claw, he sent several of the zombies flying, bones clattering on the ground.

Rikar's satisfied growl echoed through the cavern amid the sounds of battle, then fell silent as the scattered bones skittered across the ground, pulling themselves back together into skeletons once again. "What the-?"

The others were discovering the same situation with the skeletons they fought. Eon would age each one that approached him, until they fell to the ground, nothing but dust. Then right before him the dust would reform into the skeletons that continued towards him.

Livinia was striking with her braids and the blades in her hands, leaping from skeleton to skeleton, tearing them apart. Bones would scatter and then reform.

Sav made many of the zombies disintegrate before her, barely even touching them, and they would reform on her, as well.

Kaine grabbed the arm of one of the skeletons, let his power seep into the bones, then tossed it over his shoulder towards a group that walked towards him. The skeleton exploded into the group, scattering bones that would reform just as the others had.

Allen shot energized arrows that exploded on impact, with the same results, though he didn't stop firing his arrows. John would shrink himself and run between the legs of the skeletons until he ended up in the middle of a big group, then shot himself into the air, expanded his body, and fell down on top of the group. They would be flattened and broken, but just like the others, they would reform.

Cellica flitted around the battlefield, untouched by any skeleton it seemed. She would leap, flip, and even twirl around from skeleton to skeleton. As she moved by them, they would fall apart, and clatter on the ground. So many fell as she passed, though within moments, they had resurrected themselves.

Calista stared in disbelief at what she saw. She paid no attention to the zombies that walked towards her. When one wrapped its rotting, stringy, arm around her neck, she was unprepared. It yanked her off her feet, her hands moved to the arm to tear it away from her. She landed on the ground, more zombies leapt at her, their boney hands teared at her skin. She let out a shriek, then released the phoenix to incinerate all the zombies, freeing herself.

Just as before, they reformed.

"How in Hades are we supposed to fight that?" Rikar growled.

Calista shook her head. She didn't know. The zombies surrounded them, and rather than go down without a fight, they all fought back. They won against each one, but it would just reform. They were starting to get tired; how long could they keep this up? They needed to get past these guys; they needed to stop Leva before she destroyed their friends on the ship.

They geared up for the next wave, breathing hard and feeling the exhaustion from this endless battle, the earth beneath their feet started to come alive.

"What now?" Eon's wide eyes turned to her, but Calista had no answer.

They watched while the ground beneath them moved and started to pull the zombies down, engulfing them within its embrace, until no zombie remained. Turning around they saw Bastion, Trish, and Saint holding their hands to the ground. Their faces tight with exertion, the ground rippled beneath their hands. When all the zombies were gone, the three Aggies fell over in exhaustion. Cellica ran to them, running her hands over their faces and hair. Within moments, the Aggies rose, looking refreshed. Cellica moved between them, with just a touch, they felt their energies restored.

Rikar looked at Calista. "Did you know she could do that?"

Calista shook her head. Taking a deep breath, she turned and moved forward, the phoenix, dragon, and hunter bows, glowed beneath her skin. Scratch moved from his hiding place to jump onto her shoulder, standing proud. Time for the final battle, the Aggies had ended this small skirmish, now they headed for Leva.

They emerged from the cavern corridor into a vast, hollow chamber, and there stood Leva.

She was nothing like Gaia, or Jaru. She was immense, her towering form nearly scraping the ceiling, as if the dying planet itself had risen to confront them. There was no beauty in her shape, no trace of perfection, like her siblings. Her body resembled a colossal, rotting tree; split, cracked, and hollowed by decay. Arms of dried, compacted mud hung heavy at her sides, ending in bony, claw-like fingers that were more suited for tearing worlds apart than touching them. What might've been her skin was nothing more than dead earth and fractured stone.

The chamber began to glow, a sickly, ominous light that bled from the walls. Leva's laughter slithered all around them, echoing; high, broken, and unmistakably unhinged.

"You're just in time," she crooned, her voice grinding like shifting tectonic plates. "You get to witness the death of your little friends and their fragile ship."

Their gazes snapped to the far end of the chamber, where the stone peeled back into a living projection of the sky. Stryx's dragon ship tore through the space beyond it, locked in combat with the Ancients. Several enemy vessels already burned and spiraled into nothing, but Stryx's ship bore deep scars as well, its hull ruptured, and its movements sluggish

"One beam," Leva continued as if discussing tonight's dinner menu rather than the fate of those fighting in space. She tilted her head, clumps of dead roots shifted and cracked while she smiled. A jagged and joyless smile. "And poof. Gone."

"You'll destroy your own Ancients as well," Calista said, horror sharpening her voice. "You defied your father to protect your children. You fought for them. You can't..." Calista started to falter as the feeling of despair rose within her. "You can't just throw their lives away."

Leva's laughter exploded through the chamber, wild and merciless, ricocheting off the walls until it drowned out every other sound. The light intensified, flooding the room with an oppressive heat that pressed against their skin.

"Children," Leva sneered. "Such a sentimental word for such insipid little creatures." Her voice dropped, heavy with rage and madness. "They are tools. Nothing more. Tools are meant to be spent and used, not coddled."

The glow surged even brighter. Pain flooded through the chamber as if the planet itself were tearing apart. The light shot outward, screaming through the void.

"NO!" They all screamed out in horror.

The ships never stood a chance. One by one, they

disintegrated; metal, flame, and life collapsing into blinding nothingness.

Calista dropped to her knees, breath torn from her chest as the light faded. Her hands shook as she lifted her gaze back to Leva. "You killed them," she whispered. "You even killed your own children."

Leva shrugged, the movement slow and careless, sending flakes of dried earth cascading from her shoulder. The indifference in the gesture burned hotter than the destruction itself. Scratch fled Calista's shoulder, skittering for cover as the rage coiled tight in her chest.

"I can make more," Leva said calmly, her voice cold as the dead world. "Once I've crushed a few pests, that is."

Calista rose, her tears drying on her cheeks, and her lips pressed together. "You won't find that as easy as you think," she spoke as the others moved closer to her, all of them poised for battle. "We have more help than you realize."

"Oh really?" Leva taunted her with that crazed smile. "You think you're little Aeternal there will help you?" A dried clawed hand pointed at Sav. "Oh, the simplistic belief that those with power would want to help anyone but themselves out."

"What're you talking about?" Calista frowned at Leva, then turned back to see Sav standing off to the side. "Sav?"

It wasn't Sav who answered, but Leva. "The

Primordial has rules for all his children, not just the Empyreans. They may all be different, but the one rule that must be followed by all, is that none of his children may fight another." Leva gave a careless shrug. "I'm already cut off and could care less, but your friend there is still tied to daddy." Her voice rose in mockery. "She won't dare to think for herself, lest she lose that precious connection."

Calista frowned at her. "The Criptines fought you, he allowed that."

Another crazed laugh bounced off the walls. "He allowed them to fight my children, not me," Leva corrected her. "When it was realized that you insects expected them to fight me as well, they had no choice, but to abandon you, and run home with their tales between their legs." Leva's form started to grow before them. "You insignificant creatures will be fighting me on your own merits, and I promise, I won't show you any mercy."

CHAPTER 25

"You were wronged," Calista said, her voice carrying as they moved apart, careful not to give Leva an easy strike. "But you don't get to burn the universe and call it justice."

"You know nothing of what I've been through!" Leva shrieked and the chamber shook with her anger. The ground began to shift, and dead roots shot up without warning. They hurled Calista, Rikar, Eon, Livinia, and Kaine backward. Other thick, rotting tendrils lashed around Allen, John, Cellica, Bastion, Saint, and Trish, binding them in place.

Calista, Rikar, Eon, Livinia, and Kaine hit the far wall with a loud crack. Dried earth broke off and showered them as they fell to the ground. Calista looked up to see the others held tightly in Leva's roots that kept tightening. She rose, shaking off the dizziness from the collision with the wall and started off towards their friends.

"No." Livinia stopped her. "You and Rikar go for the queen. Eon, Kaine, and I will help the others. We can't keep giving her easy targets."

Calista wanted to argue as she looked at their friends, she felt as if she was abandoning them, but Livinia was right. They need to take on the queen, put her heart back where it belongs, and pray it stops her. With one final look at the others, she nodded to Livinia, and turned to Rikar.

"Shall we?" she asked him. With a single curt nod, he shifted to dragon and leapt into the air at Leva. She closed her eyes and called for the phoenix within her, letting it overtake her. Opening her eyes, she let the power loose, and flew directly at Leva.

Out of the corner of her eye she saw Eon using time to age some of the roots, while Kaine exploded others, and Livinia used her sharp braids and knives to shred even more. She had just landed on one of Leva's earthen arms, using the talons to pierce the dried muddy arm. Leva shrieked out in pain and attempted to slam her into the ceiling.

She released the arm and dove down to slice through the decayed wood that were attempting to act as Leva's legs. Rikar breathed his blue fire at Leva, burning all the dead, rotting vines and roots. Even with the damage they were inflicting upon her, she still fought and retained her form.

The whole cavern turned on them all, the ground would liquify under their feet, sinking them into the mud all the way up to their necks. Allen, Kaine, and Cellica found themselves in this position until the Aggies loosened the dirt around them enough that they were able to pull themselves out of their almost-graves.

For that, the Aggies found themselves encased within some dried-up leaves and roots that they couldn't control. It took Livinia and her blades to release them. John would change his form so much that Leva wasn't able to contain him in any trap she created. This angered her so much, she sent a giant muddy stone wall careening towards him with such force there was no way that he would be able to avoid it.

Calista shouted for John to watch out, forgetting about Leva, and letting herself get distracted. Leva grasped her within her clawed grip, squeezing her tightly, laughing maniacally as she did. Calista could only watch in horror, praying that John would be able to get out of this.

Cellica screamed for John to move, but he turned and froze, no time for him to get out of the way. Cellica turned away with a shriek, unable to watch him die in such a way. Just as the wall reached John, it turned into a bunch of colorful flying insects, and John stood there with a bemused expression on his face.

Leva turned to Sav and shrieked out, "you're forbidden to interfere, Aeternal."

Sav shrugged and grinned at her. "I may not be able to attack you directly, per the Primordial's rules. Doesn't mean that I can't help out friends that just happen to be in your way." Sav winked at John, who grinned back at her with a raised fist in solidarity.

The cavern lit up once again, blinding them all. When the light subsided, Sav was gone. Calista frowned at Leva. "You killed her? Seriously? How could you?"

"Oh, please, stop with the melodramatics." Leva stared down at Calista who glared back at her. "She's not dead, I sent her back to daddy, where she belongs." Her voice turned vicious as she continued. "The rest of you, though, will not leave my world alive." She squeezed hard, and hard as Calista tried, she couldn't shimmer from her grasp.

Rikar swooped down and blasted her arm that held Calista with blue fire. Leva let out a painful shout and threw Calista at Rikar, which sent them both flying into a nearby wall, and falling to the floor with a thunderous impact that sent dust and twigs flying all around them. They hit with such force that they could barely push themselves off the floor.

Leva let out more unhinged laughter. "You're two mighty heroes are no match for me, and now I will dispatch the rest of you." She turned to focus on Kaine and Eon who were destroying her vines that had captured Livinia. The ground around all three started to pull them down, no matter how they fought against it.

Cellica darted through all the vines that kept attempting to capture her, with a twist here, turn there, and a flip over them, she landed beside Rikar and Calista. She smiled at them, reaching down and touching them both. With each touch, they felt their strength, and energy returning.

Calista sat up and gave a thankful smile, before she launched into the air with Rikar, to attack the queen once more. The Aggies freed the others from the muddy trap while Leva growled at Cellica with displeasure. "That's not allowed, little insect. Time to deal with the consequences of your actions."

Leva's arm started to glow brightly as she pointed towards Cellica. Calista thought about the ship's earlier destruction, her chest tightened, as she flew towards Leva, knowing she wouldn't be able to reach her in time to stop anything.

The light shot from her claws, straight towards Cellica who couldn't move due to the vines that grabbed her and held her in position. Right before the light reached Cellica, John had grown in size, and stepped in front of her. His eyes widened as the light engulfed him, expanding in size, until it burst with a blinding explosion.

"NO!" The pained agony in Cellica's voice as she watched the light slowly die. There before her, on the ground, lay John. The light didn't disintegrate him, possibly due to his gift, but they could all see the life leaving him as they watched. Cellica fell to her knees, the vines gone, and held him to her as she wept.

"Such useless creatures with their pathetic emotions," Leva scoffed. "I'm done with this, time to bring your worthless existences to an end."

Calista felt the agony within her rise, she looked at

Leva, and glared. "You're right, it's time to end this." She looked at the others. "We concentrate on Leva only, time to bring her heart home."

Everyone turned to Leva, even Cellica left John to fight her. Blue fire, phoenix flames, Arcblader energy, braids and knives, all their powers and gifts were hitting Leva with the intensity of their emotions. She would shriek and lash out at them, glowing lights of energy would burst towards them, barely missing them. One nicked Kaine, though it knocked him to the ground, he got back up and limped right back into the action.

"Don't we have something that would distract her?" Rikar glared at Calista who frowned back at him, before she realized what he meant.

"Oh, right!" Calista nodded.

"So, get it!" Rikar roared as he turned to rain more blue fire on Leva.

Calista nodded and rode down on her phoenix to the ground, where Scratch ran out from his hiding place, the vials clutched to his stomach with his powerful webbing. She grasped the vials, rolling to avoid a vine that shot out at her. She attempted once again to open the vials but ended up having to dodge yet another vine.

"Forget it!" She grumbled and smashed the vials into the ground. All three essences combined with a glow that filled the room. A glow that even gave Leva a pause as she turned to stare. Calista moved back from the dust on the ground, moving to where her brother stood watching Leva.

Three figures rose from the dust, Jaru, Gaia, and Ara. Jaru nodded to Calista before he looked up at Leva who just stood there and stared at them. Gaia and Ara both looked around them in shock, though when Gaia saw Calista, her eyes narrowed.

"Leva, dear sister," Jaru spoke and moved forward, his hand held out.

"How dare you!" Leva shrieked at him. "How dare any of you betrayers show your face to me!"

Jaru paused and looked back at both Gaia and Ara, before turning back to Leva. "You're right, we did betray you. You didn't deserve the punishment that you faced." Jaru looked back at Calista, widening his eyes at her, as if to ask why she was just standing there and not moving. She gave a nod and moved to Eon while Jaru continued speaking to Leva. "I'm sorry, and I know that saying sorry isn't enough to repair the damage we caused."

"Sorry?!?!" Leva reared back, her head hitting the top of the cavern, raining down dirt and dead roots on top of all. "You think sorry will take back all the damage that you've caused?"

Eon reached into one of his many time folds and pulled out the heart of Leva. He watched Leva and the visions of the other Empyreans as he handed the staff to Calista. She nodded and moved slowly to stand near Leva while she was distracted.

"Leva." Ara moved forward, looking up at her sister.

"We were wrong, we know this, but what you've done to our children is inexcusable."

The room shook as Leva peered down at Ara, the anger that radiated from her was almost suffocating. "Did you think of my children when you betrayed me to our father? Did you think of how the excommunication would affect them?" Her voice rose, the cavern shaking with her anger.

Calista used the distraction to launch herself towards the queen, landing on her chest and pressing the heart against her breast. As soon as the heart touched the queen, it absorbed itself into her. The queen let out a piercing scream and knocked Calista back, then fell to her knees, still screaming.

Calista rushed back to stand with the others who watched with wide eyes as Leva held her hand to her chest, where the heart started to glow brightly. She sent up a silent prayer to whomever was listening, that this would heal Leva. She wasn't sure they could win any other way, even damaged as Leva was, she was still highly powerful.

CHAPTER 26

Leva raised her head and looked around, Calista and the others backed away as more deranged laughter filled the air.

"I don't think it worked." Eon shook his head as he backed away.

Leva ignored them and moved towards the visions of her siblings, her laughter still filling the air around them. "You think that putting that wretched heart back into my body would stop me?" she asked shrilly. She threw out one of her arms towards Calista and the others. Instantly they were tossed against the far wall, some invisible force not only holding them there, but also pressing against their throats so that they couldn't breathe.

Calista kicked out and struggled against the invisible barrier as Leva taunted her siblings. "Come to watch your children die?" she asked them with a laugh. "You can feel how helpless I felt those years ago."

"Leva, let them go," Jaru pleaded. "You can't condemn them for our faults," he tried to reason with her.

"Silence!" She shouted at them. "You stood in silence while our father handed down his punishment to me, so now you can stand in silence while I hand down my punishment!"

Calista felt her body start to go slack, she quit fighting against Leva's hold and called forth not only the phoenix, but the dragon and hunter as well. Each tattoo started to glow and shot forth towards Leva. She reared back and lost her hold on them all, letting them drop down, gasping for breath.

"Time to end this!" Calista shouted hoarsely, grabbing her sore throat. They all moved forward, attacking Leva with all the powers they possessed. Blue flames shot out at Leva who deflected them and shot back with powerful bursts.

"Enough!"

The loud booming masculine voice shook the cavern more violently than any of Leva's shrieks. They were thrown to the ground and looked up to see not only Sav standing there but also the male from Jaru's visions. They were looking at the Primordial.

Recognition rippled through all the siblings, and while Ara, Gaia, and Jaru fell to their knees, heads bowed in reverence and fear; Leva remained standing. She glared at the Primordial with eyes hollowed by centuries of ruin, her body trembling not with fear, but fury.

"How dare you!" She spat at him.

"Careful, my daughter," the Primordial said, his voice low and immeasurable. "You stand before the one who shaped the first light. I could unmake you with a thought."

"Then do it!" Leva screamed. "Anything would be kinder than what you left me to endure while they lived beneath your favor!" The pain in her voice cut deeper than any weapon ever forged.

Calista started forward, ignoring the protests of Eon and the others. "Leva is right," she told him, unsure of where this bravery, or stupidity, came from.

The Primordial's gaze settled on her, curious rather than angry. "And who are you, small one, to speak so boldly?" he asked.

"I'm a child of Gaia by birth," Calista said, voice steady despite the terror flooding her veins, "and of Ara by love. I'm also someone who has loved and lost because of a decision that you made long ago."

"Do you know who you address?" he asked her, his head moving slightly in his confusion of someone so tiny, daring to contradict him.

"I do," she said. "And I know the truth. Leva didn't stand against you alone. She was punished for dissent that others shared, and abandoned."

"Truth?" he asked her after several moments of silence. When Calista nodded to Jaru, Ara, and Gaia, he turned to them. "What is she speaking of?"

Ara stepped forward, her voice quiet. "We must confess, father."

"I am listening." He nodded.

"When Leva challenged the laws you set," Ara said, head bowed, "the choice was not hers alone."

"She was not alone?" The Primordial stared at them.

"No," Gaia said. "We were meant to stand with her. We believed as she did. We did nothing; out of fear."

The Primordial stared at them all, then his gaze fell on Leva. "My judgement was absolute when wisdom was required. I see now that my punishment went too far." Leva said nothing, just stared at him. "Can you find it within yourself to forgive me?" he asked and Calista's eyes widened in amazement.

Calista's breath caught, but before she could speak, Rikar and Kaine pulled her back.

Leva laughed then, a sound broken and empty. "I have my heart back," she said as her whole being shook with her emotion. "And still, there is nothing left inside it. My world is ash. My existence is pain. And after all this time... you ask for forgiveness?" Her voice rose, raw and unhinged. "I will never forgive you; any of you. I will not stop until you feel as dead as I do."

The Primordial gave a sad sigh and moved forward, before Leva would do anything, he placed a darkened hand on her brow; her eyes closed and she went still. Calista stared up at Leva in amazement, then back to the Primordial.

"She lives," he said calmly, answering the fear in Calista's eyes. "She sleeps. Her mind is fractured; her grief unchecked. I will mend what I can."

The Primordial then turned to Gaia, Ara, and Jaru. "You, too, have failed her."

"Yes, father," they all intoned together, their heads hanging.

"Your reckoning will come," he said. "Not now; but it will come. This, I promise." He looked once more at Leva, his expression unreadable. "My punishment created this... but it does not absolve her of what she has done. Her consequences will be mine to bear and correct."

The Primordial turned to look down at Calista. "I grieve for what my daughter has taken from you."

"Can you bring them back?" Calista asked, her tone desperate as she thought of all those who have died because this family squabble, as Alastor called it. "They died for lies," she implored.

"No," he told her gently. "The law forbids it. Life, once ended, does not return; not even by my hand."

"But they're your laws," she argued, fighting back her tears. "Can't you bend them; just this once?"

The Primordial knelt down, shrinking in size until he stared right into her eyes. "If I bend one law," he said softly, "then none have meaning. Even creators must obey what they set into motion." Then he straightened and grew once more. "But those who are true children, such as yourself, you will see them again." The air around them started to shimmer as the Primordial spoke again. "I can send you home, if you would like."

Calista swallowed hard, trying to keep the disappointment from showing. She wanted to argue, but how do you argue with the one who created all? Instead, she asked, "Atlantis?"

The Primordial nodded. "Yes."

She yearned for home, for the simple safety of curling into her mother's arms and crying until the pain dulled. She imagined being held, comforted, listening as her mother promised that everything would be all right. For a moment, she wanted nothing more than to lean on someone else and let them carry the weight for her.

But she shook her head and released a slow breath. "Not yet," she said quietly. "We still have promises to keep. Lives we swore we'd return for. They deserve to know the war is over." Her voice wavered as the truth settled in. "We just… need a ship." She didn't let herself think about Stryx or the crew. The ache in her chest was already too sharp.

"That," the Primordial said, "I can help with."

The world around them flared with blinding light and when it faded, they stood on the bridge of a ship unlike anything they'd ever seen. The Primordial's voice echoed through the pace, resonant and final.

"Go. Fulfill your promises."

Calista stood on the balcony of her temple, watching the comings and goings around Atlantis. She felt hollow inside, even though her mother and others had done their best to help ease the pain she carried. She had cried, no, she had bawled her eyes out. Sobbed for hours, until her face was full of red blotches, and her eyes puffy. No pretty crying like you see in the movies, just heart wrenching sobs that filled her temple.

They had kept their promise; they found the refugees of Ara. Those that wanted to return to one of the moons, they helped to facilitate that. She looked down and saw Velva walking down one of the pebbled paths with Rowena. Some returned to Atlantis and made their home here, whether it be in town with the mortal residents, along the river in their own camps they made, or here with her fellow deities.

Velva had been welcomed by Rowena to stay in her temple; they had become close friends. Velva would go down to the camps by the river at night, and by their campfires, she would tell the stories of not only Ara, but Calista and those who fell in the war with Leva. Brooke and Allen made their home in the camp, while Kaine found a room in her parent's temple. Her father had come to like him, they would sit and talk about Solen, when they didn't think she could hear them.

Bastion, Saint and Trish had only stayed long enough for the remembrance ceremony that was held for those who had lost their lives in the senseless war. Calista had stood next to Rikar while the images of those they had lost had been brought to life by Atmos and his acolytes. At the base of the mountain, an eternal fire burned in the hearth, bathing the statues of those who had been taken from them in its light.

Bastion, Saint, and Trish had left colorful flowers from Ara at the feet of Sanders. Shaylane and Brax left colorful trinkets in the palm of Trelaine's statue. Calista saw Brax place one in the pocket of Alastor's when he thought no one was looking. Velva cried at her brother's statues, where they stood, their hands locked together in a permanent show of brotherhood. Cellica leaned against John's statue, silent tears flowing. There were flowers and gifts of all kinds placed around the crew of their ship, Stryx, Clori, Clyde, Clare, Bern, Arlo, Tanis, and Lissy. Messages of all kinds were placed around the memorial; we'll be together again, our heroes, we love you, all useless words that meant nothing to Calista.

She couldn't look at any of them, she felt she had failed them all. Kaine had tried to get her to see Solen's statue, but she refused. Rikar stood at Draken's statue and didn't move, for how long she didn't know. When she finally left the memorial, he still stood there.

It had been several days since the memorial. She had said bye to Bastion, Saint, and Trish as they left for the moon of Ara to be with their families. Saint and Trish told her that Grager had left the small meteor of Jaru's with the other Picknies who had decided to go home. They didn't know if Jaru had stayed there with Eryx, Lantis, and Cleeves.

She wasn't sure she cared.

A movement on the rail of the balcony caught her eye, Scratch was watching her. He hadn't left her side much since he'd been reborn, and since coming home. He helped to wipe any tears, but now, she had nothing left to cry. He had been exploring Atlantis, though he stayed close by, in case he was needed. If he wasn't in her temple, she knew she could find him in her brother's.

"Still here, I see." She turned to smile at Eon, who joined her on her balcony.

She leaned into him and nodded. "I am." She looked to her right and grinned at the newly broken-in land. "I see you've chosen where you want your temple."

He nodded and grinned. "I have." Gave no other explanation, not that she needed one. "Rikar and Livinia have left. He said they needed to find their home, and he needed some space."

Calista swallowed hard and nodded. "I understand."

"Give him time, sis," Eon told her. "He'll come around, it will be just like old times soon enough."

She nodded, though she didn't truly believe that. Experience taught her that once something was broken, it was never the same again. All any of them could do was to live their lives the best they could, remember those who had fallen, and wait until they could walk with them again.

"Are you going back to the mortal world?" She heard the hesitation in her brother's voice, as if this question was one he hadn't wanted to ask, but the answer was something he needed to hear.

She looked over towards the mountain, where the

statues would stand forever, and the fire would never go out. She gave a shake of her head. "I'm home, and home I will stay, until it's time to join Solen."

"I hope that isn't anytime soon," Eon said, watching her closely.

She gave a slow shake of her head and sighed. "I made him a promise, and I will keep that promise." She leaned into her brother and closed her eyes. "I always keep my promises."

Note from the Author:

You didn't think I would leave the book like that did you? There is more to tell and a story that needs an ending worthy of an Atlantean Princess. Calista's story isn't done yet, and I have a surprise for everyone. The finale will be told by none other than Paul Bush. He has a vision for the ending that I agree with, and he wanted to be the one to tell it to everyone.

So, sit back, and listen to the finale of Calista's story … Spider's End.

PAUL BUSH

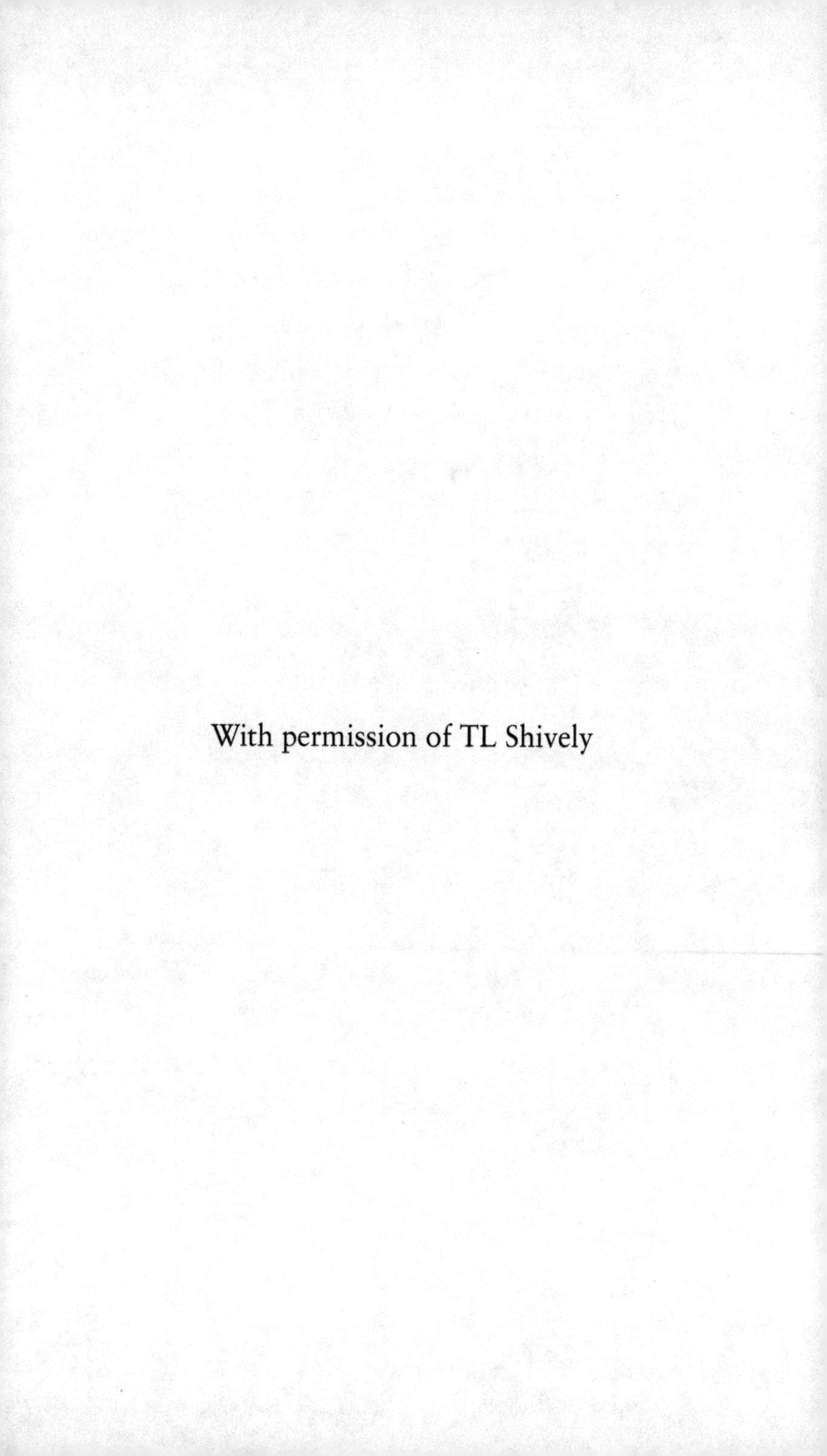

THE SPEAKEASY

Riker sat alone at the bar, staring into the amber depths of his drink. He raised the glass to his lips and took a slow sip. It had a sweet but warm taste despite having ice in the glass. He took another drink, this time finishing it and setting the glass down on the bar. Riker motioned to the bartender for another. The bartender, John, set the glass he was drying on a shelf of the bar and slowly walked to the other end and reached for Riker's empty glass.

With a clinking sound of more ice being added to his glass, John looked Riker in the eye and asked, "Do you want another? Or have you had enough?"

"I'll have another, thanks." Riker watched as John made him another drink that he had named after himself. A John Stahle. It was bourbon mixed with ginger ale. But, at this point, it was mostly just bourbon.

This was the anniversary of the day Draken, his older brother, died. Struck down by a weapon Riker's own stolen energy powered. The Ancients had drained Riker to fire it. Draken had pushed a fellow comrade named Kaine out of the line of fire, taking the blast himself. That blast had struck Draken in the chest, delivering its deadly blow.

Riker could still remember watching as the light faded from Draken's eyes. He could still feel the pain of that day as if it were mere moments ago. Today, as with every year prior, is the day Riker would come to this bar and raise a glass or two in remembrance of his brother.

"I thought I would find you here," came a familiar voice from behind him.

Riker didn't even turn around. "Haven't seen you in a while. And, you were the one who introduced us to this place, remember?" Riker said coldly as he set his empty glass on the bar.

"That your first? Or have you been here a while?" Calista sat down next to Riker and motioned to John for a drink. "Mind if I have one with you?"

Riker looked over to John. "Can we get two more, John?"

"So, how have you been?" Riker said, making an attempt at small talk.

"I've been good. I've been spending time at home in Atlantis," Calista said. "My parents and brother were wondering when you and Livinia were coming for a visit."

Riker chuckled, "Now there's a switch, you asking me when I'm coming home. Not that it was ever really my home. Remember, I'm the son of a Greek God."

"You know my parents always thought of you and ..." Calista's voice trailed off.

"Can't say his name? Draken. You mean they thought of Draken and me as family, right? But we were just trapped there because of the curse," Riker said, sounding colder.

"And because of that curse, you were welcomed into a family who loved you both. And after all, wasn't it a Greek God that caused the curse in the first place?" Calista's voice started to sound as cold as Riker's.

Riker turned and looked at her. His face started to soften. "I'm sorry, Calista, I know Draken's death was not your fault. And I do also still miss Solen. Ahh…the times we all had," Riker said softly.

"You mean all the tricks you played at my expense?" Calista laughed.

"Not always. There was the time Draken and I turned Cael and Malis's home into a water bomb minefield full of lobsters and crabs. Unfortunately, Malis arrived home before Cael. Your mother was so mad." Riker laughed. His mood started to brighten. "I've never seen the Atlantean God of War so mad at anyone in my life. I thought for sure she'd turn us into throw rugs."

Just then, Sav walked up with their drinks. "Sorry, John had to step out for a few. Is there anything else I can get you?" Sav said, looking at Calista with a smile.

Calista let out a low shriek of excitement and threw her arms in the air. "SAV! We haven't seen you in so long! How have you been?"

As Sav came from behind the bar, Riker and Calista embraced her. The three of them pulled out chairs from a nearby table and sat down.

The three of them were lost in memories of the last time they'd all been together. Glasses lifted in quiet tribute to absent friends and family.

As they finished their last drinks, the door to the bar burst open.

Kimi stormed inside, breathless. "Riker—he's gone!"

Riker shot to his feet and caught her shaking hands in his . "Who's gone?"

"Calton!" Kimi cried. "He's vanished. I think he stowed away on the last ship bound for Ara."

Silence fell over the table. Since the end of the war, ships had come and gone for the moons of Ara, where family and friends lived. With each flight, they would stop on the planet to report back whether Ara had fully healed or not.

Kimi then turned her gaze on Calista.

"You," she said, her voice tight with fury. "What are you doing here?"

"Last I knew, you didn't have dibs on this place, and if anyone did, it would be me anyway," Calista said curtly.

"Kimi," Riker raised his voice to her. "This isn't about Calista; let the past go. Draken's death wasn't her fault. Now, tell me, what makes you think Calton has left for Ara?"

"He's been spending time with the refugees from there. The other night, Calton said he was going to see the last ship take off for Ara, and now he is nowhere to be found."

Draken stood and looked at the table. "Calista? Is Kaine still in Atlantis?"

"Yes, he is," Calista replied.

"Go, have him gather everyone and get his ship ready. I'll go and tell Livinia what is happening. We may need her tracking abilities to find him. If Calton is headed to Ara, then he plans to kill Lisbet. He told me that he had been listening to the storytellers from Ara, and that he blames Lizbet for Draken's death. Over the years, I have tried to get him to let it go. Telling him that these things all happen for a reason. And that the anger he was holding on to would someday destroy him. I had thought I had finally got through to him."

With that, Calista nodded and shimmered out.

ATLANTIS

"Kaine," Calista shouted. "Get the ship ready. We need to get to Ara as fast as we can. Kimi believes that Calton stowed away on the last ship headed there. He plans on killing Lizbet."

Just then, Riker, Livinia, and Kimi appeared. Kaine stood and nodded to Riker.

"I'm on it. Give me an hour. Be ready for lift-off."

With that, Kaine pulled a small radio from his coat and spoke into it.

"All crew members to the ship and prep for take-off. We're headed home."

Kaine then ran off in the direction of the ship.

Kimi turned to Calista. "This is not your fight. Stay home."

"Go to Hades," Calista replied coldly.

Calista's voice rose in anger. "I loved Draken as much as anyone. I was there to watch as the light vanished from his eyes. And I'll be damned to sit by and watch his son get hurt or possibly die trying to avenge his father. So, get out of my way, or I'll plant you where you stand!"

Calista closed her hand into a fist, energy forming around it. Readying her stance to strike at Kimi.

"KNOCK IT OFF!" Riker shouted at Calista and Kimi.

"We don't have time for this! Our main goal is to get to Ara, find Calton, and bring him home safe! After that, the two of you can go somewhere and have it out for all I care once and for all!"

Calista dropped her hand, and the energy disappeared. The words Rike shouted at her and Kimi cut deep. After all these years, did Riker still hold her responsible for what happened to Draken? Was that why Riker avoided her since they got back home after the death of the Queen?

"Calista." The sound of Riker's voice brought her attention to him.

"Go tell Malis and Cael what's happening. And get back here as soon as you have." Riker ordered.

Calista nodded. Turning away from Riker so he wouldn't see her eyes start to water at his words, she headed for her mother's temple.

Malis, Cael, and Eon stood as Calista entered her mother's temple. Malis gave a puzzled look at her daughter. "Cali, what's wrong?"

"Kimi believes she and Draken's son, Calton, stowed away on the last ship headed for Ara. He'd been listening to the Ara storytellers about how Draken died. She believes he blames Lizbet for Draken's death and plans to kill her. Kaine is prepping the ship for takeoff. Riker is taking Kaine's crew to track Calton down and bring him home. Kimi and Livinia are with him. I'm going to help them." Calista explained.

"I'm going as well," Eon stated.

"Eon," Cael looked to his son. "With the passing of your grandfather, you're next to succeed him and are needed here in Atlantis."

Eon's eyes darkened, and his gaze dropped to his left shoulder. There, sitting very still, was Scratch. Since the passing of Tylaos, Scratch had been spending a lot of time with Eon. Sensing that Eon needed comforting from the pain he was feeling over his grandfather's death. This brought joy to Calista. Knowing her best friend and her little brother were creating a bond like the one she had with Scratch.

Looking up at his father, Eon spoke.

"Dad, I know Atlantis needs a ruler, but I'll not stand by as my sister puts herself in danger. I have to help her. It'll be difficult for her to go to Ara. The memory of the two people she loved the most may be overwhelming. I don't want her to deal with that without me. And I loved Draken as much as she did. He was like the older brother I never had. And I cannot stand by and let Calton possibly die trying to avenge his father."

Cael looked at his son, pride swelling inside him. "You take care of yourself, son. Go and bring Calton home. And watch out for your sister."

With that, Cael hugged his children, kissed them both on the head, and turned to look at Malis.

Malis embraced Eon. "You're just like your grandfather, always the protector. I love you. Be safe and bring Calton home to us."

Malis then turned to Calista. "Cali, please follow me. I need to have a word with you."

Malis led Calista to the next room of the temple. The pictures on the wall were of Calista as she grew up in Greece. And then after she had returned home to Atlantis. Malis stopped and turned to Calista and spoke.

"Cali, these pictures of you bring me both pain and joy. We watched as you grew from Rowena's pool, unable to help you when you needed us the most. My heart would hurt more and more each day. But when Solen returned you to us, it was like a joy I'd never felt. Now I worry about the path you're going down. Once again, I'll not be able to help you when you need me."

Malis reached her hand out and took Calista's forearm as if to shake it. She drew her daughter closer, placing her other hand on the two arms. As Malis's hand started to glow, she looked into Calista's eyes.

"Cali, we'll always be connected. I'll always know when you're in need. I love you more than you'll ever know. We'll always be a part of each other. Know that I'm so very proud to be your mother and of the goddess you've become. Always helping those who would need you. Now go and do what you feel you need to do," Malis said.

Embracing her daughter, eyes swelling with tears, Malis whispers, "goodbye, Calista, Goddess of Manipulation, until we're together again."

TIME FOR TAKE-OFF

As Calista and Eon approached Kaine's ship. Scratch jumped from Eon to his mistress's shoulder and nestled into Calista's hair. She felt the warmth of his little body. But something felt off with him. Like it would be the last time he did it.

But Calista looked over and smiled at him and said, "Hello, Scratch, good to have you back."

"Scratch was a great comfort to me when granddad died," Eon said, looking at his sister. "Thank you, Scratch, and thank you, Calista, for everything."

Calista looked up at her brother and smiled, "I love you, Eon, never forget that."

Calista hugged Eon. Releasing him, she smiled and said, "Let's get on board before Riker decides to leave us."

Entering the bridge of the ship, Kaine moved to greet them. "About time you guys showed up. I was beginning to think you weren't coming." Kaine smiled as he shook Eon's hand. Then he turned to Calista.

"Are you going to be ok going back to Ara?" The worry on Kaine's face was clear.

"I'll be fine," Calista said, putting up her hand to stop any other questions from him.

Draken had pushed Kaine to safety when the Ancients fired their weapon at him, taking the full brunt of the blast and saving his life. That was a debt that Kaine could never repay. Now he would surely give his life to save Calton, Draken's son.

"Calista, Eon, let me introduce you to Gnome. He was one of the champions we saved during our fight with the Ancients. Don't let his size fool you. He has a fighting style that rivals even Livinia's. Gnome is one of the best to have by your side. He doesn't talk much but will definitely have your back in a firefight," Kaine said. "He's also our pilot on this trip. One of the best, so get prepared for the space fold. We leave shortly."

They both nodded to the smaller male, who only grunted, barely acknowledging their presence. Not much hair on his head, though his silver and black beard was plentiful. Purple bandana wrapped around his forehead with a silver scythe that glinted. Eon pressed his lips together as he looked at Calista, who just shrugged.

As Eon and Calista passed through the crew's common area of the ship, they were greeted by two familiar faces. Allen and Brooke smiled and hugged them.

"Damn good to see you both," Allen told them.

Brooke, still hugging Calista, said, "It has been too long. We'll have to not let that happen again."

Standing next to Brooke was Cellica, smiling at

Calista. They hug. Flashing back, Calista's memory of when John died protecting Cellica from Leva, the hurt in Cellica's eyes reminded her of her own pain when Draken and then Solen were killed. The war with the ancients took so many good people, leaving behind all those who loved them.

"Good to see you again, Cellica. How've you been?" Calista asked.

"I've been doing okay," Cellica replied. "Kaine and his crew have taken me in and have treated me like family. They gave me a purpose to go on after John's death. Something I desperately needed. And how have you been?"

"I've been ok, staying home in Atlantis. I took up keeping the records of Atlantis. I spend most of my days reading all the old scrolls and books. Arranging the treasures in the cave and getting to know all of its history. Becoming somewhat of an expert on it," Calista said.

Just then, Riker and Livinia entered the room.

"Everyone, we lift off in 5 minutes and will space fold right after. Get into the hibernation pods." Riker ordered. He nodded to Eon but avoided looking at Calista.

THE ARRIVAL

Calista felt nauseated as she opened her eyes. After all the times she did it, it still turned her stomach.

Eon opened her pod. "How are you feeling, sis? Are you going to be ok?"

Calista sat up slowly. Waving her brother off, "I'm ok, Eon. I just have to get up and move to clear my head. It's been a while since I've done this."

Calista looked around. "Have we arrived at Ara?"

"Yes," Eon replied. "Everyone is preparing to land. Come on, we have to gear up. Ara is still in pretty bad shape."

Just then, Riker entered the room.

"We're setting down near Sala Way," Riker said, voice tight. "Livinia caught a flash on the scopes; energy signatures. She's sure someone is fighting down there. It may be Calton. We think he has found Lisbet already and is trying to kill her. Gnome is going to do a fast landing with the bay doors open, so be ready to move." Riker ordered.

Then Riker looked at Calista with concern in his eyes. He opened his mouth as if to say something, then turned around and took off to the rear of the ship. What was that, she thought to herself.

"Let's move, Eon. I'm not going to let Calton die at the hands of Lizbet," Calista said, rushing past her brother, her eyes blazing.

The name hung in the air like a challenge, sharp and final; there would be no turning back now.

Riker and Livinia were the first to the doors. Just as the doors started to lower, Riker grabbed Livinia and jumped. Falling through the air, Riker transformed into his dragon form and landed on the ground with a thunderous crash.

Eon brought the rest down from the ship in a sphere like the one used when rescuing them from the Ancients all those years ago.

Once on the ground, Riker transformed back, and Eon let the sphere fade away.

"Calton!" Kimi yelled.

Riker looked at the battle being waged in front of them. It appeared that Lizbet was getting the better of Calton. Knocking him to the ground, wielding a glowing spear, and as she raised it over her head to strike the fatal blow, she saw her: Calista. Eyes wide, fire in them, Lizbet screamed, "YOU!"

THE BATTLE

Lizbet reached down and pulled Calton to his feet. Standing behind him, she raised the blade of the glowing spear to his throat and glared at the group bearing down on her and yelled, "Stop!! Or this pathetic little one dies!!"

Riker grabbed Kimi and ordered everyone to stop.

"If you hurt him, nothing will stop me from ripping you apart!" Kimi yelled.

Lizbet smiled at her. "You think so? You could try. But you see, this blade glows with the remaining power of Ara. And it has the power to kill even a goddess." Lizbet's eyes narrowed at Calista.

"Let him go, Lizbet," Calista ordered. Closing her hand, energy formed around it. Calista knew that spear; it was the remaining heart of Ara, the same one they saw in Jaru's visions. She knew it was powerful, that it connected the mystic to the Empyrean. Whether or not it could kill a goddess, she wasn't sure, but that fact wouldn't stop her from ripping Lizbet apart if he harmed a hair on Calton's head.

"Keep her talking," Kaine whispered. "I'll get Calton to safety."

Lizbet's smile widened. "I've waited so many years for this day. The day you'd return so I could get my revenge. You took everything from me. My home, the man I loved, and now I'm going to return the favor. Starting with this one!"

Pushing Calton forward, knocking him to the ground, Lizbet raised her spear to strike. Just as she intended to strike, from the side, Kaine charged Lizbet. Pushing her sideways. But as she fell, she swept at Kaine's leg, knocking him to the ground.

As Kaine started to get to his feet, Lizbet was on him. She struck him in his face and knocked him to the ground once again. This time, pointing the glowing spear at him, she laughed.

Calton lunged, his blade flashing as it slashed across Lizbet's arm, drawing a bright arc of blood. Lizbet screamed in pain and swung back in a furious counter-strike, but Calton tucked and rolled, the blow cutting only empty air where he had been a heartbeat before.

He came up on one knee beside Kaine, gripping his shoulder and hauling him upward. "On your feet," Calton said through clenched teeth, eyes never leaving Lizbet as she recovered, wounded but far from finished.

Lizbet lunged forward, and Calton, like his father once did in the heat of battle, pushed Kaine aside, bracing himself for the killing blow Lizbet intended for him. Calton's eyes look to his mother.

"NOOOOO," Kimi screamed.

But the blow never came.

Instead, Calton felt a sudden overwhelming rush of power surging around him, hot and blinding. His eyes flew open. A brilliant flash of light erupted outward, and with it, a phoenix of pure fire and radiance unfurled around them, wings spread wide in a deafening cry. The shockwave slammed into the ground, hurling Kaine back and throwing Lizbet clear, her scream swallowed by the roar of light. Calista had shimmered in front of Calton just in time, taking the deadly blow meant for him.

The sudden silence crashed down just as hard.

Calton staggered backwards, disbelief etched across his face. He turns and meets Calista's eyes. For a heartbeat, neither of them spoke.

Then his gaze dropped.

A glowing spear of energy protruded through her chest, its light pulsing. Time seemed to fracture as Calton's world narrows to that single, impossible sight and the horror of realizing the power that saved him may have come at a cost he can never repay.

At the exact moment the spear tore through Calista's back and burst from her chest, lightyears away back in Atlantis, Malis gasped, clutching her chest. A crushing pain seized her heart, and as she cried out in pain only a mother could know, she dropped to her knees.

"Malis!" Cael rushed to her side, catching her before she fell completely, his arms wrapping around her. "What is it?" he asked, fear already tightening his voice.

Malis clutched at his robes, tears spilling freely now as she looked up at him, her eyes shattered with certainty no words could soften. "Our daughter is gone," she whispered.

The words struck harder than any blade. Cael pulled Malis close, holding her as her sobs broke free, his own breath hitching as the truth settled over them like a burial shroud. Together they remained there on the cold stone floor of Atlantis, locked in grief, mourning the loss of their daughter, lost to them once more, as cruel as the first time, but this time it would be final.

THE RECKONING

Hissing, Scratch leaped from his mistress's shoulder toward Lizbet as she returned to her feet. As he landed on her chest, Scratch sank his fangs into her skin. Lizbet let out a scream. Pulling Scratch off her and throwing him several feet from her.

"Wretched beast," Lizbet spat out, pulling a dagger from her belt. "I will carve you to pieces and leave you lying next to your mistress!"

As Scratch's venom starts to blur Lizbet's vision, time seems to stand still around her. But as her sight had begun to refocus, she saw Eon. Standing in front of her, she strikes at him. Eon avoids the attack and grabs Lizbet by the forearm. Lizbet's heart started to beat rapidly. Years of life became like minutes. Lizbet's skin started to wrinkle and turn gray. She looked into Eon's eyes as he spoke to her. "This is for killing my sister," Eon spoke coldly.

Lizbet screamed, but the sound faded as the accelerated time turned her old. When Eon released her, only her corpse remained.

THE LAST GOODBYE

Moving to return to his sister's side, Eon knelt beside her, and tears flowed down his face. He took her hand as she raised it to him.

As Calista lay in Riker's arms, she looked up to Eon. "My little brother. Not so little anymore." She smiled at him. "You're starting to look more like our grandfather every day, you know." Eon gave a half-hearted smile, kissing her hand as he clutched it to his face. "Please take care of Scratch. See to it that he always knows that he meant the world to me." Calista breathed in painfully and gave a watery smile. "Tell our parents that I love them, and I will see them again." He nodded, tears falling, though he stayed silent.

Calista looked up to Riker. As he tries his best to hold back the sobs, Riker gives her a half-hearted smile, tears flowing freely down his face, "Hey there, princess." Calista could not remember the last time he called her that. She looked at him and smiled.

"I love you, Riker. You and Draken were always picking on me, but I knew that you both loved me and would always be there if I needed either of you. I always felt your love for me. My two protectors," she smiled. "I had to save Calton for Kimi. She shouldn't lose both her husband and her son to the same vile person."

Calista looked to Calton, "Take care of your mother." Calton nodded to Calista. Looking at Kimi, "He looks a lot like his father," Calista told her. With no sound in her voice, Kimi mouthed the words thank you to Calista.

"Riker, please tell Zeus that his granddaughter forgives him. And that I love him. And the next time you see that bastard Aries, knock him on his ass and tell him his "daughter" says goodbye."

Riker snorted a laugh as he sobbed. Holding her close to his chest. Calista's voice was weakening; she looked to Livinia. "Take care of Riker, he's just a big kid, you know. Always needing to be looked after." Livinia nodded to her, wiping away the only tear that Calista ever saw fall from her eyes.

As the light faded from Calista's eyes, the hunter's symbol glowed brightly on her chest and faded away. Kaine looked down, touching the symbol as it appeared on his chest. Then a warmth of power rushed over the group. A blue dragon came spinning down around Calton and Kimi. The tattoo of the dragon appeared on Calton's chest and arms. Calista's eyes seemed to weaken, and then suddenly, a fiery phoenix filled the sky. Power rushed over the land. Bathed in the power of this phoenix, the land started to revitalize. The waterfalls started to return, and plants were growing all around. The hole in the center of town was once again a beautiful pool. A glowing figure rose from its center, moved toward the group, and bent down next to Calista.

"Solen," Calista's eyes filled with tears as she spoke his name.

Solen smiled at her, "Spider," he said. "You have healed Ara. She'll once again be as beautiful as before. Her people may now return to her. And I've come to take you to Aetherfall to be with our friends and myself for the rest of eternity. We'll never again be apart." With that, the light faded from Calista's eyes for the final time, and they closed.

As the spirit of Calista rose from her body, Solen embraced her with a deep, loving kiss. She was once again in his arms, looking up into his eyes, smiling. For the first time in what felt like forever, Calista was happy again.

Solen then turned to his brother Allen. "A life given, a pain that burns, a hazy vision, and life returns. Go tell our people to come home. Ara welcomes them back with open arms."

"I will, brother, I will," Allen told him. "I love you, Solen."

Moving to stand next to Kimi and Calton, Riker held Livinia in his arms. Another glow came from the center of the pool. It was Draken.

He smiled down on his son. "I'm so very proud of

you, son. Know that I will always love you and your mother. Take care of her for me. And look after your uncle, he needs all the help he can get." Draken smile at Calton.

Looking at Kimi, "You were not my second choice, you know. You were the one I chose. I love you, always, never forget that." Draken said, touching her cheek to wipe away the tear that fell from her eye.

Draken, turning to Riker, "I'm proud of you, little brother. I'll always be with you, here." Draken said, placing his hand over Riker's heart. "When you need me, look for me there."

Turning to Solen and Calista, Draken hugged them both and said, "Let's go home."

The three of them floated over to the pool and descended beneath it and vanished for the last time.

THE END

The sun was just starting to set as the group made their way back to the ship. Gnome, standing guard at the ramp of the bay door. Looking to Kaine, he said, “noise all over communications. Ara’s people know she’s healed, and they are coming home. In fact, I think some are here.” Gnome pointed to the sky behind them. A ship descending on the field not too far from them landed. The bay door opened, and people slowly came out, rejoicing that they were finally home.

Rikar took Livinia in his arms and kissed her. Livinia looked at him and asked, “Where to now?”

Riker looks at the people from the ship and then at her. Only one word comes from him.

“Home.”

ACKNOWLEDGMENTS

I want to thank my wife, TL, for trusting me with something so deeply personal to her, Calista's story. *Spider's Awakening* was meant to be a standalone book, but after I read it, I knew that it couldn't be one and done. The story had more to say. Calista had more to endure, more to become. I pushed for that continuation, and she agreed, on the one condition that I help write it with her.

What followed was hard work, late nights, long conversations, and moments of frustration. But also laughter, discovery, and a kind of joy over something that we were creating together. And somewhere along the way, the truth settled in my head that every story, no matter how beloved, must eventually end. When I asked if I could place *Spider's End* at the close of the third book, she said yes. That act of trust means more to me than I can put into words. Thank you for believing in me, for sharing this journey, and for loving me. I love you more than these pages can ever express.

To my older brother, Norwood, I've looked up to you my entire life. Even when we didn't always see eye to eye, you were always there when it mattered most.

We may not say it enough, but I love you, and I'm grateful for everything you've done for me.

To Douglas Pierce, Eric Hawkins, Brian Morris, Jean Davis, Robert Mendenhall, Stefanie Gilmore, and to every creative soul we've met while traveling from convention to convention. Your passion, your stories, and your kindness mattered so much to me. You may never know it, but you helped shape this journey. You inspired at least one soul, and that inspiration will carry forward long after the final page is turned and the book is closed.

To all of our friends who allowed us to weave pieces of themselves into Calista's story. We thank you for trusting us with that honor. We love you all.

Saint, please don't yell at Sinner.

About the Author

TL Shively writes YA fantasy with a twist, including her debut novel, *The Guardians*, and later, the *Spider Trilogy*, which was her own personal challenge to herself, turning her fear of spiders into a story about Gods and Aliens. Fueled by her mother's encouragement and whimsical tales of childhood imaginary friends, she has been crafting stories since grade school. When not working on new stories that explore different realms of fantasy, TL enjoys spending time with her husband, family, and friends, whether playing cornhole or exploring their home state of Michigan.

OTHER BOOKS BY AUTHOR

Sanctuary Guardian Series Reading Order:
The Secret Sanctuary
The Town That Time Forgot
The Battle of Sleeping Lady
The Independence Mine Disaster
The Hunter's Betrayal
Haven's Shadow
A Sanctuary Christmas
Echoes of Arcadia

Spider's Trilogy:
Spider's Awakening
Spider's Return
Spider's Vengeance

Also from author:
Sanctuary and Friends coloring book

www.ingramcontent.com/pod-product-compliance
Lightning Source LLC
La Vergne TN
LVHW091113080826
845145LV00008B/1900

* 9 7 8 1 9 5 2 3 2 5 2 2 9 *